ACT 1

by Andrew Keenan-Bolger
and Kate Wetherhead

Grosset & Dunlap
An Imprint of Penguin Random House

GROSSET & DUNLAP
Penguin Young Readers Group
An Imprint of Penguin Random House LLC

Cover illustrations by Avner Geller and Kyle Webster.

Library of Congress Control Number: 2014045697

ISBN 978-1-101-99522-8   10 9 8 7 6 5 4 3 2 1

IN LOVING MEMORY
OF JACK NAVIN

Chapter

One

−JACK−

"Please, no show tunes right now," I moaned from the cave of boxes in the backseat.

"Not even *Into the Woods*?" my mom said sweetly, plugging her iPod into the blue stereo cable. "Stephen Sondheim always puts you in a better mood."

"No, you can just listen to NPR or something," I grumbled.

My mother twisted around to get a better look at me from the passenger seat. She placed a cool hand on the side of my face, then brushed a strand of hair off my forehead. I pulled away from her touch, burying my face deeper into the cardboard den.

"Suit yourself," she said, sitting back, unplugging her iPod, and spinning the radio dial.

The car stereo hiccuped fragments of country music and static as I sat stewing in the backseat. Honestly, I would have *loved* to listen to *Into the Woods*, and my mom was totally right: All it took was a few harmonies and clever rhymes from the opening number, and a grin would instantly curl up on my face. I'd discovered the musical a few years ago on a trip to the New York Public Library. My dad, a firm defender of physical books and music, was browsing the old CD section when my nine-year-old eyes fell upon a snazzy album cover—a forest of trees, the largest of which formed into a wolf's head growling down at a pack of frightened cartoon figures. Taking it for some fairy-tale recording, my dad checked it out, not realizing he was unlocking a lifelong obsession with musical theater for me. I remember listening to the finale, a tear-jerking "Children Will Listen," and deciding that *Into the Woods* was the closest thing I'd come to magic.

Since that day, I'd listened to hundreds of cast recordings, and while shows like *Next to Normal*, *Cabaret*, and *Gypsy* got plenty of playtime, *Into the Woods* would always be my most treasured. Its composer, musical-theater superhero Stephen Sondheim, would become my favorite writer, and my dream role would become the character Jack, which, as luck would have it, happened to be my name.

I tried stretching my stiff legs underneath the jars of flaxseed and wheat germ my mom insisted on bringing with us. *"Who knows if our new town will have a health-food store?"* I rested my sneakered feet on an overstuffed pillow of chia seeds as a man's nasally voice filled the car.

"Today on our program 'Taking the Leap': stories of people who took big risks and gained unexpected riches."

I yawned. Listening to the cast recording would certainly have put me in a better mood, but the truth was, I just didn't feel like being happy right now. If I'd learned anything from *Into the Woods*, it's that when your fairy-tale wishes came true, Act 2 would come along and spoil everything. I was supposed to be starting the seventh grade at the Professional Performing Arts School, an awesome place that packs its day not only with math and science, but also with dance and acting classes.

I was supposed to spend my days off in New York City, picnicking in Central Park and eating ice cream on the Hudson River. I was also supposed to become the thing in life I'd always dreamed of being: the star of an original Broadway cast. A green road sign swiped by my window proclaiming "Cleveland: 302 Miles"—further proof that none of these things was going to happen.

I wasn't your typical twelve-year-old. While most kids my age spent their evenings studying plant cells and watching bad reality shows, I spent my nights memorizing lines and performing on Broadway. I'd been in two and a half Broadway shows: *Mary Poppins*, *A Christmas Story*, and the half was complicated and the main reason I was stuck in a backseat, wedged between boxes of dishes and my dad's *National Geographic* collection.

"How long until the next rest stop?" I asked. "I'm getting hungry."

"There's one in Harrisburg, but unless you want Starbucks for lunch, it looks like we should hold out till Altoona," my dad said. "Think you can wait a couple hours?"

Al-tuna, I mouthed. My stomach rumbled with the thought of avocado sushi rolls and salty vegetable dumplings. "I can wait."

"You know, Nana was telling me last week that they just opened a Dave and Buster's not too far from the new house," my mom said, turning down the radio volume. "Shaker Heights has a lot of the same places as New York."

"Do they have a Staten Island Ferry?" I mumbled sarcastically.

"What was that?" she asked.

"Nothing," I said, leaning my head on a Sharpie-marked box. "Wake me when we get to Al-Tuna."

Closing my eyes, I tried to replay the final memories of my last day in New York—the morning sun creeping up the street like a summer fire-hydrant puddle, the screeching of metal as my dad rolled the door to the U-Haul shut, my mom's good-byes to Marcel, the guy who worked at the corner store, her arms loaded with coffee cups and bagel sandwiches. Everything had looked different. The sidewalk, usually crowded with strollers and dog walkers, was as empty as our living room. The Upper West Side soundtrack of car horns and multi-language cell-phone chatter had been replaced with an eerie early-morning silence.

I caught my reflection in the grease-smeared window of our minivan. My favorite shirt, once baggy enough to tuck my knees under at the breakfast table, now seemed to be hugging my shoulders a little too tightly. They were right. I was changing.

Change was something most twelve-year-olds couldn't wait for. When will my voice sound as deep as my older cousin's? When am I gonna be tall enough to ride Kingda Ka at Six Flags? When can I get my first tattoo? Okay, not so much that last one. But when you're a kid working on Broadway, change meant a final curtain call, a return to everyday kid life.

That spring I had been cast as the lead in *The Big Apple*, a new Broadway show about a kid and his mother who go from singing on subway platforms to headlining on the Great White Way. On the first day of rehearsal, I knew something was wrong. The notes that had been so easy to pop out in the audition only two months ago felt strained. I chalked it up to nerves, but even when I got home that night and practiced, it felt like the high notes were getting stuck in my throat. The next day I was in a full state of emergency. What if I cracked on my high note? What if my understudy was better than me? When was the creative team going to find out my secret: Their star was growing up?

"Ugh, sorry. I'm just getting over a cold," I remember saying to our music director.

"No sweat, Jack. We can work on it some more tomorrow."

My dad's voice startled me awake. "Wake up, Jack Sprat. We're in Altoona."

The food selection at the rest stop was hardly an improvement over Harrisburg's. I forced down a slice of pizza topped with mushrooms and a puddle of neon grease. After picking up some magazines at the gift shop, we loaded back into our U-Haul-hitched minivan. Mom's talk radio was replaced by a loud-voiced conversation with my dad, obviously meant to be overheard by me.

"I just can't believe the good timing. A position opening up in the Cleveland Regional Transit Authority, just minutes away from your mom's house."

"The schools in Shaker Heights are supposed to

be some of the best in the nation."

"It's going to be good for Jack to finally have a backyard to play in."

I stayed silent for the rest of the trip, not even piping up to ask how many kids in Cleveland have Central Park down the street from their house. After a seemingly endless stretch of flat green land, I saw a sign reading "Exit 151: Cleveland."

I began to make out buildings in the hazy distance. As we drove up a ramp, the skyline came into view. Like New York, the city overlooked a body of water, but with only a handful of skyscrapers, it looked more like a Christmas tree lot than the vast Manhattan forest of steel.

"Jack, you see that tall building with the golden spire?" my dad said, gesturing toward my mom's window. I remained silent. "Yeah, well that's Terminal Tower. It was built in the 1920s and was once the fourth-tallest building in the world. At night it's lit with yellow lights and glows just like the Empire State Building."

My dad was a nut about history and geography. I was usually amused by his monologues on long road trips, his rambling on about how such-and-such architect went blind late in life or how so-

and-so used to name his bridges after childhood pets, but today his perky energy felt more like a punishment. Back in New York he worked for the Metropolitan Transit Authority. They were the people who looked after the city's subways, buses, and trains. Consequently, the Goodrich family never took cabs. *Ever.* Even last June when my family got tickets to the Tony Awards, my dad insisted that we ride the subway, tuxes and all. *"Nothing gets you where you want to go faster than a New York City subway,"* he always declared. Both Mom and I knew how badly Dad wanted to be the head of his department, so this spring when he was passed over in favor of someone a lot younger, the whole family felt the blow. This news became further complicated when a call arrived announcing that the city of Cleveland was overhauling their transit system and was looking for someone to run it. My dad began dreaming aloud at the dinner table, pondering how great it would be to run his own department and return to the town he grew up in, but with his son about to star in a new Broadway show, his dream stayed a dream.

"Do you see that big glass pyramid?" my mom

chimed in. "That's the Rock and Roll Hall of Fame! Your dad took me there the first time we went home for Thanksgiving at Nana's. Remember that picture in front of Elvis's jumpsuit?"

My dad smiled, placing a hand on my mom's knee.

"How long until we get to the house?" I asked.

"We're approximately nine miles from the house," my dad answered. "Try counting down from"—he tapped his fingers on the steering wheel, pretending to use an invisible calculator—"one thousand two hundred and fifty."

I made sure he was watching in the rearview mirror as I rolled my eyes, all the while secretly counting down in my head, *One thousand two hundred forty-nine, one thousand two hundred forty-eight* . . .

Around nine hundred fifty-something I gave up, noticing an abrupt change in scenery. Hitting exit 160, we pulled off the expressway and onto a tree-lined street. It was crazy how quickly the factories and office buildings gave way to identical-looking tan-brick houses and frozen-yogurt stores.

"It should be up here on the right," my dad said, placing a map against the steering wheel.

"Jack, look at it! It's our new subdivision!" my mom squealed, practically levitating from her seat.

I looked up at a dazzling sign with curlicue gold writing: "Sussex Meadows: Like Nothing You've Ever Seen." We began driving down a winding row of brown and beige houses, each one bearing the exact same lawn, the same window shutters, the same Mercedes SUV parked in the driveway, and an American flag hanging over every front doorway. My dad pulled up in front of an impressive but unmemorable house and began to back the U-Haul trailer up the spotless driveway. I got a sinking feeling in my stomach as I realized they were right—this was like nothing I'd ever seen.

Chapter

−LOUISA−

Never had a stretch of highway seemed so bleak.

Four and a half hours had passed since my parents picked me up from camp and my eyes were still puffy from all the tearful good-byes. The *only* thing making me feel remotely better was the original-cast recording of *Into the Woods*, which we'd already listened to earlier in the trip. As we drove beneath a sign announcing "Shaker Heights: 30 Miles," I reached across the cup holders to turn up the volume, seeking comfort once again in the musical's opening number, in which classic fairy-tale characters sing about what they want.

"I wish
More than anything
More than life
More than jewels
I wish . . ."

My dad reached for the volume dial and cranked it back to the left, abruptly silencing the music.

"I'm sorry, is it just me or do all these songs sound the same?" he asked, gesturing at the stereo.

I gave him my most disdainful look. No one at camp would have ever asked such a question.

"They do not all *sound the same*." I sighed.

How could my own dad not hear what made *Into the Woods* amazing?

He only heard repetition, while I heard wit, anticipation, and hope. I had listened to the original-cast album hundreds of times, and there were still parts of it I had a hard time singing along to— Stephen Sondheim (my favorite lyricist/composer) was like a magician with music. You know when you're listening to a song and you think you know how the tune's going to go? It wasn't like that in a Sondheim song. He tricked you. But the genius part of it was that the unexpected still felt right.

"C'mon," Dad teased, *"Into the woods, and out of*

the woods, and back to the woods, then out of the woods again . . ."

"That's not what it sounds like!"

It was obvious that we were nearing the end of our drive home because my mood was going from mopey to downright cranky.

"You just don't appreciate the complexity of Sondheim," I muttered.

Dad looked at me, eyebrows raised. I could tell my big words had impressed, or at least surprised, him. Still, he wasn't about to give in.

"I 'appreciate the complexity' of a turbine engine," Dad said with a smirk. "*That* is complexity worth appreciating. This Sondheim stuff sounds like a record skipping."

Horror.

"It does not!"

I made a dramatic sound of disgust. Dad laughed.

From the backseat there was a rustle of newspaper as my mom chimed in.

"Lou, don't listen to your father. He doesn't know what he's talking about."

"You don't think I know how a turbine engine works?"

"That's not what I meant, and you know it," Mom said, swatting Dad's arm.

I twisted around in my seat, grateful for an ally in defending my beloved show.

"Thank you, *Mom!*"

She winked at me.

Mom preferred to ride in the backseat on long car rides so she could spread all the sections of the *New York Times* across her lap. After four and a half hours, she'd exhausted all her favorites and was now reading the Automobiles section, which I knew did not interest her. I'm sure she was happy for a momentary distraction, even if it was to act as referee between me and Dad.

"Well, that's what it sounds like to me," Dad said, a little grumbly.

"You really don't like it?" I asked him, baffled. The opening number to *Into the Woods* was one of the most amazing, most epic pieces of music I'd ever heard.

"I like Sheryl Crow better."

Okay—he had his taste, I had mine.

"Can we just finish listening to the opening number?" I pleaded.

"I think that's fair, don't you, Doug?" Mom asked, the Automobiles section obscuring her face.

"Fine." Dad sighed, clearly outnumbered. "Lou wins. But when it's over, we're switching to Sheryl."

"Deal," I said, and returned the volume to its earlier level.

Listening intently to Cinderella wish for an invitation to the Prince's ball, the Baker and his wife for a child, and Jack for his cow to give milk, I wanted—*"more than anything"*—to add my own voice to the recording:

"I wish camp had lasted forever!"

In reality, it had only lasted a week. Still, it had made quite the impression.

Camp Curtain Up (CCU, for short) was designed specifically for people who loved musical theater—meaning it was designed specifically for *me*. I had been bugging my parents for two years to let me go, and that summer they had finally agreed, putting money aside and driving across Michigan to drop me off at a place that could only be described as *paradise*. Tucked away in the woods by a beautiful lake, CCU offered an intense week of musical-theater training: scene study, song interpretation, voice and acting technique, tap, jazz . . . basically, everything I wanted to do, all the time. But the best part of CCU was that it was the first (and only) place I'd ever been where every single person was exactly like me.

We were all Musical Theater Nerds (MTNs, for short). We wore this title with pride at CCU, where for one perfect week, obsessing over how high Idina Menzel belted in *Wicked* was not only acceptable, it was encouraged. We could debate endlessly about whether the original-cast recording of *The Last Five Years* was better than the movie-cast recording (it was), and no one looked at us as if we were weird. We didn't have to convince one another that *Into the Woods* was sacred. Everyone at CCU knew that it was.

It's not like I didn't have friends at home; I did. But no one appreciated the things I was passionate about, certainly not with the same intensity. Even my closest friend, Jenny, who'd been taking ballet since she was five, kind of zoned out if I went on for too long about Kristin Chenoweth's impeccable comic timing.

There were the Shaker Heights Community Players, who had cast me as Amaryllis in their production of *The Music Man* last fall, but they were all much older than me. (Even the role of Winthrop, the little boy who sings "Gary, Indiana," had been given to Amy Judd, a petite fifteen-year-old girl with short hair.) I'd had a lot of fun doing the show with the Players, but I didn't really consider any of them my *friends*—it's not like I would have invited any of them over to hang out at my house. (Though Amy Judd did babysit me once when my parents went out for their anniversary.) Besides, the musical they'd chosen to do this fall was *Chess*, and there were definitely no roles for kids my age.

"*I wish—*"

I was snapped to attention by the crystal-clear voice of Little Red Riding Hood, played by Danielle Ferland.

My parents were discussing what to do for dinner, and I shushed them.

"Just till this part's over," I said, "please." And

then I couldn't help but sing along.

"It's not for me
It's for my granny
In the woods
A loaf of bread, please"

Having listened to the album so many times, I knew every word, every inflection, every breath that Danielle Ferland took, and I made sure to match her as best I could.

"You really do sound just like her, Loulou," my mom said once the solo was finished.

I know moms have to say stuff like that, but I still loved being compared to Danielle Ferland. Little Red Riding Hood was my dream role.

"We have similar vocal placement," I said, using a singing term I'd learned at camp.

Mom leaned forward and looked at me as she rested her head against the driver's seat.

"You know, Lou, I've said this to you before, but you are very lucky that you've figured out so early in life what you love to do. It'll be challenging, for sure, but some people spend their whole lives searching for something they're passionate about. You're only twelve years old and already set."

"Yeah," I said, looking out the window.

I wanted Mom's words to make me feel better, especially since I knew how much she meant them. She hadn't figured out what she wanted to do until a couple years ago, and was now (at age thirty-nine) about to start her third semester studying psychology as a part-time student at Cleveland State Community College. All the same, a wave of self-pity washed over me as we passed a "Shaker Heights: 20 Miles" sign. Having just said good-bye to a bunch of people who loved the same things that I did, I felt incredibly lonely as I pictured myself back in my normal life. I'd looked forward to camp for so long, and now that it was over, I had nothing to look forward to except seventh grade. Blech.

"And home before dark!"

The prologue to *Into the Woods* was over, and true to my word, I switched out my iPod for Dad's, scrolled down the Artist list to Sheryl Crow, and seconds later we were all listening to her proclaim that she just wanted *"to soak up the sun."* Dad sighed with contentment. Mom reached from the backseat and patted his shoulder.

"You're a good father, Doug."

Dad took the Northfield exit, signaling the last ten-minute stretch of our journey home. Even though there were still two weeks remaining before I would become a seventh-grader, it kind of felt like the summer was over. I stared out the window as the increasingly familiar landscape—Thistledown Racino, Heinen's grocery store, and Pearl of the Orient (Dad's favorite Chinese restaurant)—turned the past week, full of dance combinations, up-tempos, improvisational exercises, and lots and lots of laughter, into a dream. The next two weeks would be full of new sneakers, haircuts, and figuring out bus schedules.

Soon enough we were taking the right off of the service road into Sussex Meadows, our subdivision, where the Thompson kids were kicking around a soccer ball in the street before their parents called them inside for dinner.

"Car!" they yelled, and scrambled toward the curb to let us pass.

"Dinner," my mom announced, revisiting the subject, "is going to be pizza. I don't feel like cooking after that long drive."

"No argument here," said Dad.

"How 'bout you, Lou?"

"Pizza's fine," I murmured, suddenly distracted by the large U-Haul parked in the driveway two houses down from ours. As Dad pulled into our driveway, I watched a woman about Mom's age carry a crate of glass canisters (holding what looked like sawdust) up the walkway and disappear through the front door. Moments later, she reappeared, followed by a kid who looked about *my* age. He was short with a cool haircut. He seemed about as interested in unpacking that U-Haul as I was in unpacking our Subaru.

"Looks like the new neighbors have arrived," said Mom, gathering up her newspaper. "We'll have to do introductions at a time when we haven't all been sitting in cars for half the day."

"Are you saying I smell bad, Hannah?" Dad said, shutting off the ignition.

He got out of the car and made grunting noises as he stretched. Mom wasted no time grabbing as many of my bags as she could carry and headed toward the house. She hated clutter, which meant that the suitcases and duffel bags were usually emptied and stored in the basement within the first thirty minutes of our return. I was ready to help maintain Mom's record, but as I emerged from the passenger side, I was caught off guard by the new kid's T-shirt, which read very clearly, "Mary Poppins." I recognized the logo from the Broadway Playbill Jenny had brought me after her family saw the show in New York. *Was my new neighbor an MTN?*

Chapter

-JACK-

The house looked like something you'd build in a computer game—one of those simulation ones where you created a character and moved them into a neighborhood. Everything felt entirely too neat. The roof slanted into perfect gingerbread triangles. The windows were framed with clean white wood and hugged by brown shutters. Bushes dotted the garden with the precision of a mouse click. At least in the computer game, your character got to be a doctor, rock star, or mad scientist. I'd be lucky if I got to be anything other than a bored twelve-year-old.

"Jack, could you grab the door for me?" my mom

called. I looked up to find her nervously clutching a table lamp, a mop, and a bag of high heels. She looked like that picture of the Cat in the Hat, recklessly balancing all those household objects; all that was missing was a fish bowl.

I slung the duffel bag off my shoulder and pulled open the screen door.

"Thanks, love," she said, brushing past me. "Can you even believe it? The house is so much bigger than I'd imagined! Wait until you see the backyard!"

I wonder if we have a swimming pool? I thought, tossing the duffel bag into a pile accumulating by the door.

My dad emerged from the back of the U-Haul carrying our coffee table covered in bubble wrap.

"I told you that website wouldn't do it justice," he called to her. "And this lawn is so huge we'll probably have to hire a gardener to keep it from turning into a jungle."

"Or maybe it's time a certain son of ours started earning that allowance." My mom grinned, setting down her stuff and jogging past me to help my dad with the table.

"Wow. You guys don't waste any time, do

you? 'Welcome to Ohio, here are your chores,'" I grumbled.

"We're just teasing, Jack," my dad said. "No talk of chores until *after* we finish unloading all this stuff."

I scuffed my feet down the stairs and made my way back to the U-Haul. Grabbing a box filled with sheet music and theater books, I began to hear my parents laughing and chattering on the porch. As I got closer, I heard them joking in exaggerated Midwestern cartoon voices.

"Golly gee, what's for dinner tonight, Dennis?" My mom giggled. "Sloppy joes and brats?"

"I reckon we better drive down to the pizzeria and pick up some slices," my dad answered gleefully. "This kitchen is so huge I'm liable to get lost in it, dontcha know?"

"Yah, yah, you betcha!" My mom chuckled.

Who were these strangers that body-snatched my parents?! You betcha? In the twelve years I'd known these people, I'd never heard them carry on like this. My parents were edgy New Yorkers. My mom wrote a food blog and my dad said things like "Ugh! Tourists!" and "My guy at the cheese shop." I wouldn't go so far as to describe them as *serious*, but *I* was supposed to be the one in the family who cracked the jokes and talked in character voices. And what was the big deal with everyone wanting a huge house, anyway? For as long as I could remember I'd heard everyone complaining about the size of New York apartments. They were always the butts of jokes on TV and in movies. *"Her apartment was so small, it was like living in a box of Cheerios."* I'd always thought of our apartment as being just big enough. I had my own room. I knew where everything was, and if it ever got tight, I could always walk a few blocks to the coolest park on earth.

I lived in a neighborhood called the Upper West Side on 86th Street. In New York a lot of the streets were named with numbers instead of words. I liked to think it made everything easier. If you ever got out of the subway and didn't know where you were, you'd only have to walk one block before realizing the numbers were going in the wrong direction. Our apartment was one of forty in the building, another perk. On Halloween, you could hit up forty different homes without even having to put on a jacket. I never had to walk up any stairs, because we had a fancy elevator. We even had our own doorman, Nelson, who'd help us with heavy groceries and give great restaurant recommendations.

As the sounds of my parents' laughter trailed to the back of the house, I set my box down and took a seat on the warm concrete steps. I couldn't help thinking about my New York bedroom. I wondered what it would look like with other people's things in it. Men were probably in there right now slapping paint over the dark green walls, whitewashing away the memories of my first twelve years. No one would remember how I'd felt waking up in that room on Christmas morning, or what it was like staying up past my bedtime, memorizing the lyrics to "You Can't Stop the Beat" from *Hairspray*. And they'd certainly never know how happy I was sitting on my bed five months earlier, reading the script for *The Big Apple* for the first time.

"So, Jack, what do you think?" my mom had asked. "The show must be pretty good to keep you inside on your first day of vacation."

Even though spring in New York usually had

me scarfing down breakfast so I could meet my friends on the High Line, I had spent the entire morning holed up in my bedroom.

"*I love it!*" I exclaimed, slapping the script shut and sliding it next to me.

"Oh good!" my mom chirped as she made her way from my bedroom door to the bed.

"You have to read it next. It's, like, really funny for the first half, and then in the final scene I got kind of sad, but not like '*West Side Story* someone dies' sad, just, like, you really care about them by the end."

My mom's eyes twinkled as she reached over to straighten the collar of my shirt.

"Do you think they'll make a cast recording?" I asked her.

"I don't see why not." She smiled.

My body hummed with excitement. I'd memorized the words to what seemed like a hundred Broadway albums and had always been in such awe of the kids who'd gotten to sing on them. Like Daisy Eagan from *The Secret Garden*, who at eleven years old (even younger than me!) won a Tony Award for her performance as Mary Lennox. I had played that album so much that I could even tell you exactly where she'd chosen to breathe in her Act 2 opening, "The Girl I Mean to Be." Would other kids be memorizing the choices I decided to make?

"I'm saying it now, Mom: *The Big Apple* is gonna be the best show of the year!"

"I hope so. That's what Davina is telling us, at least."

Davina was my agent. She was the person who let my parents know when I had an audition or who booked a job, kind of like a school guidance counselor, but instead of talking about classes, it was conference calls, coffee, and contracts. She was a short, sturdy woman with curly silver hair and a loud, thick New York accent that I always thought made her sound like Bugs Bunny. Her voice carried so much you could hear her talking on the phone while you were still in the elevator. She pronounced *New York* like *Noo Yawk* and *theater* like *theet-uh*. She was what my dad called a "tough cookie." On the whole, I really liked her. Plus, she always sent me edible fruit arrangements for my opening nights.

"You know this is going to mean you'll have to have a tutor for the months you're in rehearsal," my mom said.

Tutoring meant not getting to hang with my school friends, but it also meant learning at my own pace and getting to eat snacks during spelling tests.

"Fine by me," I answered. "I think we should tell Davina we're in!"

"I think so, too, Jack . . ."

"Jack. Jaaack. JACK!"

I jolted back to reality. My parents were standing at the top of the steps, concerned looks spread across their faces.

"Do you want to take some of this stuff up to your room?" my mom said, pointing to the pile of bags and boxes. "You've barely set foot in the house."

"Oh sure," I said quickly, pushing past them and into the entryway. Our living room was big and white with uncovered windows. A light smell of lemon lingered from the hardwood floors, still glossy from whoever cleaned them last. A grand staircase sloped from the living room up to the second floor. It reminded me of that scene in *The Sound of Music* where the Von Trapp children stand on the stairs and sing "So Long, Farewell," the musical theater equivalent to "99 Bottles of Beer on the Wall." I grabbed my backpack and dragged my feet up the stairs.

"Jack, your room is down the hall on the right," my dad called after me.

I made my way down the dark hallway and stopped at the last door. I could see tape residue in the center of it from where the previous resident must have hung something, an art class picture or maybe a No Parents Allowed sign. I pushed open the door. The room was flooded with light from a big window facing the backyard. My eyes did a quick scan as I stepped in. No swimming pool. Beneath my toes I could feel a dent in the carpeting where the foot of a bed once stood. I crouched down and sprawled out on the floor, bathing in the warm rectangle of light from the window. I stared up at the freshly painted ceiling.

"My name is Jack Goodrich," I said to myself. "I'm from Shaker Heights, Ohio, and this is my home."

It felt like reading lines from a strange play; one I knew I had to start memorizing. There was no turning back at this point. My parents had already fallen in love with the new house. They were already planning dinners with Nana and the cousins, whose names glowed dimly in my memory. Soon there would be rugs rolled out on the floors and photos hung on the walls, letting the world know that the Goodrich family was here to stay. There would be no more numbered streets and subway rides to school. There would be no more dance classes on Mondays and auditions in tall buildings. And there definitely would be no phone call from Davina explaining that it was all a big mistake, that the director had gotten it wrong and needed me to come back to save *The Big Apple*.

"Jack!" I heard my dad bark from downstairs. "Come help us with the mattress."

Chapter

Four

–LOUISA–

I was no anthropologist, but I was pretty sure you didn't wear a Broadway-show shirt unless you were a fan of the Great White Way. *Who is that kid?* I wondered as I sat on my bedroom floor amid bittersweet reminders of the last week: scripts, sheet music, leotards, tap shoes, a signed Playbill of *Jersey Boys* (my voice teacher had been in the national tour, so I had him sign my program). Maybe it was because I was still grieving the end of camp that I was so fixated on the boy in the *Mary Poppins* T-shirt, but I couldn't help think what a nice consolation prize it would be to have a neighbor with similar interests.

Mom appeared in my doorway. "Darks first," she instructed, placing a laundry basket next to my yoga mat. The countdown to "Camp Curtain Up: Like It Never Happened" was well under way. I must have been making a face, because Mom said, "I'm not asking you to *do* the laundry, Lou, just *separate*." And she was off, calling after my father, "Do you have any darks you wanna throw in, Doug?"

I started picking through my dirty clothes, wafts of Coppertone and OFF! rising from the mound. Such a mundane task required music, I decided, so I grabbed my iPod out of my backpack. The Broadway-cast album of *In the Heights* seemed like the perfect choice—its funky Latin hip-hop beats would provide just the right amount of spice. As Lin-Manuel Miranda delivered his rapid-fire lyrics, I thought: Rapping. There's another skill I would have to master in order to work in the American musical theater. And writing, too, since Miranda not only starred in *In the Heights*—he wrote it. I felt a rush of panic as I contemplated how much I would need to learn to be ready for Broadway. And how one week a year with Broadway professionals (if I was lucky) just wasn't enough. I thought of all the math and science classes that would take up precious time in the years ahead—time I'd much rather spend in a dance studio, or at a voice lesson, or in an acting class. My mind drifted once again to my "Mary Poppins" mystery man, and I wondered if he felt the same frustration. Seized by curiosity, I hastily threw my dark clothes into the laundry basket and carried it downstairs to the kitchen, where I found Mom on the phone, a Donato's takeout menu spread in front of her. She placed her hand over the receiver as I set the laundry basket at her feet.

"I'm getting two pies, Lou. One with just cheese and one with sausage and peppers. That okay?"

"Sure," I said, "I'm going out for a sec."

"Have you finished unpacking?"

"Almost done. I'll be back really soon."

"Lou—"

"I promise!"

I headed down the hallway and out the front door, a girl with purpose. But once I hit the sidewalk, I realized I had no plan. What was I going to do? Walk right up to the kid's house, knock on the door, and ask him what his dream roles were? If he could do a triple time step?

No, I thought. *Better to just observe, at first.* Which really meant spy. That would be hard to do in a subdivision, though, where dark alleys and shadowy corners were hard to come by. If I'd been old enough to drive, I could have just parked the car a short distance from the kid's house and crouched beneath the dashboard like the detectives did on television: a stakeout, I think they called it. But the best I could do at this moment was stay on the *opposite* side of the street, as if that was going to make me seem less obvious when I walked slowly by the house, staring like some creep.

I counted down the sidewalk squares as I approached: eight, seven, six, five . . . Why was I so nervous? Maybe because the thought of finding an MTN *on my block* was too thrilling to imagine. Except I *could* imagine it: geeking out about the new Elphaba replacement in *Wicked*, singing along with Audra McDonald's new album, making Tony Award predictions, writing our own fake Tony Award speeches . . . What was I doing to myself? I didn't even know this kid's name, and already I'd made him my new best friend. It was too much pressure—for both of us. But I kept walking. The U-Haul was still there, with the back open and a metal ramp bridging the trailer bed and the driveway. No people were in sight, however, so I sat on the curb and killed time by retying the laces of my sneakers. The sound of a screen door opening grabbed my attention, and I looked up to see who must have been the new kid's dad walking out of the house and toward the back of the U-Haul. He caught my eye and gave a slight nod and smile before striding up the ramp. *Okay*, I thought, *I've been spotted.* What now?

The dad reappeared carrying a large black-framed mirror, and as he approached his front stoop he called into the house, "Hey, can somebody open the door for me? My hands are full!" A few moments passed, then a hand appeared from inside, pushing the screen door out toward the stoop. There he was, the "Mary Poppins" kid. As he stepped aside to let his dad in the house, he looked right in my direction. I froze. My stomach gripped—he'd seen me. As I considered running away and abandoning "Mission: Expose MTN," both father and son disappeared behind the screen door. They must not have gone too far inside, though, because I could hear the dad speaking encouragingly: "Across the street . . . about your age ... C'mon ... shouldn't ... so shy."

No kid likes to be told how to make friends, and I felt a little embarrassed for my new neighbor as he begrudgingly reopened the door and peered out, uncertain. Something about the expression on his face, an odd mixture of intrigue and sadness, made me wave. Just a slight raising of my right hand and a curl of the fingers. He walked hesitantly out onto his stoop and waved back.

"Hey," he called across the street.

"H-Hey." The simplest word ever got stuck in my throat. I tried again.

"Welcome to the neighborhood," I said. "My name's Louisa, but everybody calls me Lou."

"I'm Jack," he replied.

"Is that short for John?" I asked, thinking we could connect through having nicknames.

"No," he said, "Jack's actually on my birth certificate."

Okay, never mind.

"Where are you from?" A safer question.

"New York City."

My heart did a backflip into the splits. He was from my favorite place in the world!

"Wow, really? I love it there."

Praising Jack-not-John's hometown seemed to have won me some points, because he was now ambling across his front lawn toward the sidewalk.

"You've been?"

Uh-oh, I thought, as I got a better look at his face, *he's cute*. It wasn't just the haircut. Even though that made me slightly more nervous, I decided it was now acceptable for me to cross the street. I tried to convince myself that something resembling normal was taking place.

"To New York? Yeah, a couple times," I replied, like going to the cultural capital of the world was no big deal. Like I hadn't squealed with delight the first time I walked through Times Square, or practically fainted when I got a picture with Tony Award–winner Norbert Leo Butz in front of Schmackary's Cookies. Exposing my inner geek was a delicate process. I needed to at least attempt to be cool.

"I never saw *Mary Poppins*, though." I pointed to his T-shirt.

Jack looked down at his shirt as if he forgot he was wearing it. His cheeks flushed.

"Oh," he said, "I was just wearing this for the

move." He cleared his throat. "Have you seen any shows in New York?"

"Oh totally," I said, a little too enthusiastically. "We saw *Matilda* on one trip. And *Cinderella* and *The Lion King* on another."

Jack nodded approvingly. "Those are all awesome."

I guess you saw all the Broadway shows if you lived in New York City. I felt a surge of jealousy just thinking about waking up every day in Broadway's backyard. Shaker Heights was a far cry from the Big Apple.

"Why'd you move *here*?" As the words came out of my mouth, I realized there was a snarky tone in my question that I had not intended.

Jack's eyes darted away for just a second, and I was about to apologize for asking what must have been a personal question, but then he shrugged and said, "My dad got a job in Cleveland." Jack looked back toward his house. "And now we're living in this totally unique house that doesn't look like any of the other houses."

Wow, sarcasm. This kid was sassy. *And he hates my neighborhood,* I thought as I took in the identical houses lining the block.

"Some of them have pools," I said, trying to be funny, but I realized quickly I might have just made Jack feel bad for not having one. He seemed unfazed.

"Pools are a lot of work," Jack replied. I wondered if this was something he'd heard his dad say.

"Hey—do you go to Shaker Heights Middle School?" he asked, changing the subject.

"I'm about to—seventh grade. Homeroom with Mrs. Lamon."

"Yeah, me too—except I'll be in Mr. Ross's homeroom."

"Oh." I didn't know whether to be upset or relieved by this news because I couldn't tell if I even liked this kid. He seemed so . . . disappointed with his surroundings. I decided to give him one last chance.

"Y'know, my friend Jenny saw *Mary Poppins*."

"Oh yeah? When?" Jack shifted his weight, putting his hands in his pockets.

"Uh, like last spring, I think?"

Jack looked toward the sky as if he were figuring out a math problem. It was weird.

"Last spring?"

Why did it matter?

"Yeah, I think April, maybe . . . ?"

"Oh." Jack's curiosity vanished instantly. I decided to ignore his weird line of questioning.

"Yeah, so *anyway*," I continued, determined to find out once and for all whether my new neighbor was a fellow MTN, "Jenny liked it, but she didn't *love* it."

Jack suddenly stared straight at me.

"Why didn't she love it?"

Okay, now we're getting somewhere, I thought. *He has an opinion about* Mary Poppins.

"Well, I think she was expecting it to be more like the movie," I said, feeling a rush of excitement as Jack's nostrils flared.

"It's actually a lot more like the *book*," he said, pointedly. "Does Jenny know *that*?"

"Probably not," I said, as my heart did cartwheels of joy, "but I do." I smiled proudly, ready to seal the deal of our new friendship.

Jack looked at me curiously. He didn't say anything, just shuffled his feet a little. I had been expecting a different reaction.

"So, uh, when did *you* see it?" I asked, hoping to get him back on track.

"Uh, I didn't see it, really," he said softly. "I was in it."

An asteroid landing on my house could not have shocked me more.

Chapter

−JACK−

Her face looked like she'd just swallowed a gumball.

"You were in *Mary Poppins*?" she asked again, brushing a strand of hair behind her ear.

"Yep."

"Well, not the original cast," she said, shifting her weight. "I mean, what's your last name?"

"Goodrich."

"Yeah, I don't remember seeing your name or picture in the liner notes of the cast album."

Wow, this girl really knew her stuff. *Liner notes?* I'd only just heard the term used this year. It was the name for the writing inside the booklet of a cast album that included cast list, lyrics, and production photos. Since music had gone digital, they were becoming a thing of the past.

"No, I was in the closing-night cast," I shot back. "The original Michael Banks is like a sophomore in college by now."

"Huh," she said, taking a step back and looking down at her shoelaces. "You're not trying to trick me, are you?" Her head snapped back suddenly. "Did someone tell you something about me? It's okay. I won't be mad, but I'd rather you just tell me now. It would save me the embarrassment of having to run home and type your name in on Playbill—"

"Why would I try to trick you?" I blurted out. "I just moved here! I didn't even know the name of this crummy subdivision ten minutes ago, not to mention the name of the resident theater nerd."

"This subdivision isn't crummy. It's the third nicest in Shaker Heights. The Goldbergs have a koi pond—"

"Okay, I didn't mean that," I cut her off. "Look, I don't know what to tell you. Either you can believe me or not."

"Hmmm," she said, crossing her arms.

I was speechless. It was safe to say this girl was

as far from what I'd imagined anyone in Ohio to be like. Not that I didn't expect at least *one* person in Shaker Heights to enjoy theater, but I hadn't banked on meeting that person approximately thirty minutes after pulling up to our new home. I looked her over carefully. Her face, while scrunched and slightly sour, was cute. Her brown hair fell just below her shoulders, wavy with warm highlights suggesting hours spent in the summer sun. Also, she was short for her grade. I almost groaned with the realization—despite the fact that this girl might be a little intense for my taste, she'd actually make a pretty good Jane Banks. *I wonder if she could sing?* Her green eyes flashed, and she began biting the corner of her mouth.

"Well, then," she said, digging her fists into her pockets and locking my eyes with a challenging stare, "prove it."

Her words slapped against me. *Prove it?* Packing up my car this morning, I knew that Ohio would mean a change of scenery, different stores and a different school. I never could have guessed that it would mean having my résumé scrutinized, my professional acting career called into question. *Prove it?* What did she want me to do? Get Davina on the phone and explain to my neighbor that I was in fact the guy I claimed to be? Suddenly an idea popped into my head.

"Fine," I said, feeling my face getting hot.

I stepped back from her and took a deep breath. I knew exactly what would convince her, something only a person who'd been in the show would know, something so tricky that I had to practice it in my bedroom, in the shower, and at the bus stop for a month before my first performance. I spread my feet apart on the pavement.

"S-U-P-E-R," I began to spell, my hands flying through the choreography. Each letter paired with its own unique gesture.

"C-A-L-I-F." The movements got faster.

"R-A-G-I-L," I sang, twisting my body.

"I-S-T-I-C-E-X-P." I whipped my arms, slicing through the thick summer air.

"I-A-L-I-D-O," I sung as the dance reached its fastest portion. My head bopped to the sharp tempo as I dotted imaginary i's on my palm.

"C-I-O-U-S," I finished, flicking my neck with a final cut-off.

I dropped my arms to my sides and looked over to Louisa. The color had drained from her face, her lips trembling as if searching for a polite response. I'd imagined this would be the time when my challenger would begin a slow clap, admitting defeat to the new kid who just threw down, but under the bright Ohio sun, on a suburban driveway, in a shirt a size too small, I realized how utterly ridiculous I must have looked. As she stood gawking in disbelief, I felt an invisible egg dripping down my face. *What had I just done?*

The silence was broken by the sound of a hundred sprinklers turning on. The neighborhood lawns filled with a mist of water as a similar wave of embarrassment washed over me. I turned around and stormed up the pavement to my house. I could feel Louisa's stare piercing into my back. I knew she was frozen, jaw on the ground, waiting for an explanation, but my heart was pounding so hard and my face was pumping with blood so hot that I didn't dare turn around. I swung open the door and slammed it shut behind me, blocking out the sounds of the sprinklers, the passing cars, and the new girl who had probably begun rolling with laughter on my sidewalk. It'd only be a matter of time before it spread around the neighborhood that the "new kid" not only brags about being on Broadway, but if prodded will perform a silly little dance. I was humiliated.

"Jack, looks like you've already made a friend," I heard my mom say from the kitchen.

I stood in shock wondering how much she had seen.

"Did I see you teaching her some of 'Supercal'? How did that come about?" she asked, entering the room smiling, carrying a stack of books.

"She, um . . . she's like a fan of the cast recording or something," I mumbled.

"That's *wonderful*! Who'd have guessed we'd move in down the street from a fellow theater lover?"

"Ask her if she wants to help carry in some of your boxes," my dad called from the basement.

I ignored him, trying to catch my breath.

"Is there a bathroom upstairs?" I asked.

"Oh, did you not see? You have your own bathroom attached to your bedroom," my mom said, setting the books next to the staircase.

"Can you believe how much space we have?"
She was glowing. For the first time I could
see how desperate she was to make me feel at
home. She was still the same mom who took me
on auditions and would celebrate by bringing
home Chubby Hubby ice cream when I booked
a job. This cornball Midwestern act she was
putting on was for *my* benefit. At the end of
the day she just wanted me to be happy again.
I managed to muscle out a tight-lipped smile
before heading upstairs.

My room was empty except for the
mattress, now lying like an upholstered island
in the middle of the floor. I walked over to a
door in the corner, what I had assumed was
another closet, and turned the handle. Once
I flipped the light switch, my eyes caught my
reflection in the mirror above the sink. My
hair was sweaty and messed up. My face was
red, a mixture of exertion and embarrassment.
My eyes traveled down to the logo on the
front of my shirt, the silhouette of a woman
with an umbrella, faded and peeling from
nights tossing in bed and countless tumbles
in Laundromat dryers. I remembered begging

my mom to buy it for me when we first saw the
show, weeks before my audition. I wore it to school
constantly and even hid it under my polo shirt
at my final callback. Until that moment, I guess
I'd considered it a good-luck charm. I grabbed the
bottom of the shirt and yanked it over my head.
I scrunched it into a ball and tossed it into the
garbage can under the sink.

Chapter

-LOUISA-

Prove it? *Prove it?!* What kind of person would *say* that? *An awful, terrible person*, I thought as I walked hurriedly down the street toward my house in a panic, horrified by my behavior. *Prove it?* I had never spoken those words to anyone, let alone a virtual stranger. I might as well have screamed "Liar, liar, pants on fire," then shoved him onto the ground. My palms were sweaty, and my heart was beating a mile a minute. I felt a fat, hot tear threatening to spill from my lower lid onto my already wet cheek. Stupid sprinklers.

I had been home from camp less than an hour and I'd already rejected its most important lessons, lessons that had nothing to do with triple time steps or breath control. They were about community, generosity, and encouragement. Not jealousy and hostility. In my head I could hear the voice of one of my acting instructors, Avery. "Louisa," she would have said, shaking her head with disappointment, "how do you expect people to support you if you don't support *them*?" I had become a poster child for What Not to Do.

You know when people say "If I could go back . . ." and then launch into a (usually boring) story about something they would have done differently? I'd never really thought about changing past events since I was always thinking about the future, dreaming about what lay ahead (opening nights and original songs written just for me by famous Broadway composers). But as I walked home, sick to my stomach, and already feeling guilty about the pizza I was sure to refuse, I was overcome by an intense desire to "go back"—to five minutes ago.

Instead of saying "Prove it" to Jack, I would have said "Start from the beginning and tell me *everything*." I would have invited him over for pizza, and I would have grilled him, in a *nice* way, about what it was like to be on a Broadway stage. I would have asked him to confirm every piece of advice given by my camp instructors. And then, because I would have been so welcoming and friendly, he might have showed me the "Supercalifragilisticexpialidocious" dance because he *wanted* to, not because he felt challenged. And I would have made him teach me every step until his parents came to get him, and I would have practiced until bedtime, determined to perfect them in the morning.

But there was no way to go back, and instead of making a new friend, I had just alienated the one person in Shaker Heights who might have understood me better than anyone. I passed a neighbor's garden gnome who sat in the middle of their soggy lawn, smirking at me through the sprinkler spray. *You blew it, Lou,* he seemed to say. I looked back at his crinkly face and thought, *You're right, gnome. I did.*

A heat wave saved me from further embarrassment before school started up again. Temperatures spiked into the mid-nineties, keeping just about everybody glued to their air conditioners instead of their lawn chairs. It was too hot to go outside, which meant I was able to successfully avoid running into Jack. I tucked my *Mary Poppins* cast recording behind my CDs of *Once* and *Newsies* and tried to convince myself that I could spend the next two years of middle school pretending that Jack didn't exist. How hard could that be, really?

Determined to bury my shame with a flurry of activity, I spent my time getting ready for school: a trip to Staples, where I was meticulous about picking out my supplies (I mean, seriously—when it comes to pens, there is a *noticeable* difference between *micro* and *fine* point). I cleaned out my closet and let Mom implement her "If you haven't worn it in the last year, it's going to Goodwill" rule. Then she took me shopping for new clothes, a somewhat depressing venture, since once again I had to walk past racks of Junior sizes and straight into the Kids' Wear section. I had really been hoping for a growth spurt during the summer, but sadly—no dice.

Even though I kept busy, I couldn't escape the

occasional reminder of my brief, though painful, exchange with Jack.

One evening, my parents, unaware that I'd ever spoken to him, devoted our entire dinner to speculating about our new neighbors.

"Mrs. Thompson says they're from New York City," my mom reported, her eyes flashing at me with expectation.

"That's exciting, huh, Lou?"

"I guess." I shrugged and casually sipped my lemonade, trying to appear nonchalant. For someone who planned on living her life in the spotlight, I must have been a pretty crummy actress at the dining-room table, because both of my parents looked at me with skepticism.

"You *guess*?" my dad asked, his tone thick with sarcasm. He turned to Mom. "Is this the same girl who has a poster of the Manhattan skyline taped to her ceiling?"

Oh yeah, there was that.

Mom shook her head in response.

"Seventh grade hasn't even started, and she's already too cool for school."

She grinned at me, knowing how much I cringed when she used outdated phrases.

"Well, I bet they're feeling some serious culture shock in *this* neighborhood," Dad said, refusing to let go of my least favorite subject.

"I'm going to give them a welcome gift tomorrow," said Mom, "a potted plant or something. You wanna come with me, Lou?"

No! Lock me in a dungeon filled with volleyballs and math quizzes for the next fifty years, but don't make me see Jack again!

"Uh, I can't. I'm going over to Jenny's."

Note to self, I thought, *call Jenny and invite yourself over tomorrow.*

"Well, you should really introduce yourself at some point. Looks like their son is about your age."

"Maybe you guys will be in some of the same classes," Dad ventured.

Unaccustomed to keeping secrets, I almost blurted out, "*Hopefully not*," but my brain sent a warning signal just in time. "Who knows?" I said, and got up from the table.

The next day, lying on Jenny's bed as she modeled different outfits for our first day of school, I told her about Jack.

"He sounds like a show-off," Jenny said, holding up two skirts at her waist. "What do you think, ladybug print or bold floral?"

"Ladybug print," I answered, envying her five-three frame, which allowed her access to the clothing racks at Forever 21. "Except Jack wasn't showing off," I continued. "He was defending himself! Because I was being a *jerk*!" I buried my face in my hands and groaned. Jenny put the bold floral skirt back in her closet and reemerged with different belt options.

"I dunno, Lou, if I told you I did ballet—"

"You *do* do ballet—"

"No, I mean if you didn't know me, and I told you I did ballet, and then you were like, 'I don't believe you'? I'd be like, 'Whatever, what do I care whether you believe me or not?'—I wouldn't do a pirouette in front of you!"

"But would you think I was a jerk?"

Jenny thought for a moment.

"Yeah, I guess I probably would."

"*See?*" I felt miserable all over again. Jenny laughed.

"Loulou, it's not that big a deal. You can't be friends with everybody. Forget about it." I sighed as she fastened a white patent-leather belt around her waist and looked in the mirror to confirm that it worked perfectly with the skirt. Almost as an afterthought, she said, "I mean, what—is he cute or something?"

I must have hesitated a second too long, because Jenny pounced on me like a Jellicle cat.

"Ohhhh, okay, I see what's going on now!" she squealed, pinning me to the bed.

"No, no, no!" I howled, though it was muffled by her comforter and sounded more like, "Mnwh, mnwh, mnwh!"

Jenny hooted with delight. I reached behind me and pinched her leg, which sent her hopping off the bed into a little jig.

"You think he's *cu-ute!*" she sang, irritatingly pleased with herself.

"I do *not!*" I declared. "I mean, he *is* cute, but that is completely different from me *thinking* he's cute."

Jenny rolled her eyes and went rummaging through her closet for shoes.

"Sure it is," she said dryly.

I realized she must be in heaven right now, since her two favorite things in life were fashion and teasing people. Ballet, while important to her, was still a distant third.

What I'd said was true, though. The fact that Jack was cute just made our interaction that much more excruciating to recount; it didn't mean I had a crush on him.

I came home from Jenny's that evening to find that the universe had been merciful once again.

"No one was home," Mom said, referring to Jack's house, "so I just left the plant on their stoop with a note."

I should have known then that the universe wouldn't be merciful forever. It always strikes a balance.

I awoke the first day of seventh grade with the familiar knot in my stomach of nerves and excitement. It wasn't the same as what I would get before going onstage; that always felt more like a twisted mop. Still, I was keyed up enough to only nibble at my multigrain waffles and then reorganize my backpack at least three times.

"I'm so glad you decided to put your highlighters in the outside pocket," Dad teased. "Keeping them in the inside pocket would have guaranteed a C-average for the year."

"Bite your tongue!" Mom shrieked, grabbing a snack-size bag of baby carrots from the fridge. Despite my intense hatred of math, I had been a straight-A student since grades first appeared on my report cards. Nevertheless, my mother was always nervous that I would suddenly turn into some kind of delinquent.

"Don't worry, Mom. Cs ain't for me," I teased, hoping my deliberate use of poor grammar would make her laugh. It did.

Normally I had to take the bus to school, but my parents always treated me to a ride on the first day. They also let me choose the music, so I decided to kick off seventh grade with some *Matilda*. (The anguished wailing of schoolchildren seemed more than appropriate.)

Eight minutes in the car and it was time. Good-byes, good lucks, up the walkway and through the double doors, and I was officially in seventh grade.

Jenny appeared magically out of nowhere, sporting the ladybug skirt we had both agreed she should wear.

"I had a feeling you'd match that headband with that shirt," she said, regarding my outfit.

"Are you saying I'm predictable?"

"I don't think I have to. Plus that's the combo they used on one of the mannequins at Gap Kids."

Busted.

"So, listen," she said, grabbing my elbow and pulling me to the left as a large eighth-grader lumbered by, "I heard there've been a couple changes to our homeroom list."

"Like what?" I asked, dodging the eighth-grader's equally large friend who followed after.

Jenny adjusted her belt, smoothed her hair, and rubbed her lips together, preparing to make her grand *Project Runway*–style entrance into our homeroom.

"I don't know exactly," she said, "but I know Steph isn't in our room anymore—she's in Mr. Ross's."

"That's too bad," I said, distracted by a gnawing feeling in my gut. Last-minute changes to our homeroom list could mean a lot more than just the loss of Steph.

And it did—I knew it as soon as I stood at the entrance of Mrs. Lamon's homeroom. With my predictably matching Gap Kids shirt and headband, highlighters nestled snugly in the outer pocket of my backpack, and the songs from *Matilda* still ringing in my ears. I understood why I'd had no trouble avoiding Jack for the past two weeks. That had only been a tease, a Post-it note from the heavens saying, "Enjoy this while it lasts." I had not set one foot inside my new homeroom and already the year was off to a very uncomfortable start: There was Jack, sitting at a desk in the front row, looking at me like he might throw up.

Chapter

-JACK-

I heard a tiny gasp from the doorway. I looked over to find, frozen, in an embroidered top and white-bowed headband, none other than my dreaded neighbor. Our eyes locked. I clenched my teeth, suddenly wishing for telepathic powers, hoping to broadcast my need for her to not blab to the class about our first encounter. But before she could get a chance to say a word, a middle-aged woman with a short haircut and Asian-looking pantsuit brushed past us.

"Good morning, class. If everyone could take a seat," the woman said, making her way to the desk at the front of the room. "Today you can sit

with your friends, your old classmates, whomever. Tomorrow I'll be assigning seats, so enjoy the freedom while it lasts."

Louisa, flustered, turned her attention to the girl standing next to her. They ducked into a pair of empty seats in the back of the classroom. I wasn't sure how much more of this I could take. I exhaled slowly, staring out the window. Rain clouds had begun to roll in, covering the bright Ohio sun. *It's just like opening night or an audition*, I told myself. *There's nothing to be afraid of.* When had a small classroom become more nerve-racking than a two-thousand-seat theater?

"I'm Mrs. Lamon, and I'll be your homeroom teacher for the year."

She began unpacking her notebook and stacks of paper from a printed tote bag with a logo reading "Women & Children First Bookstore."

"I'm also your humanities teacher. You'll come to me in the morning and then travel as a group to your other classes. This year we'll be covering the changes in history, geography, literature, and politics from AD 1600 to the present that have shaped the world we live in today."

As Mrs. Lamon continued to explain the

curriculum, I peeked over my shoulder to the back of the room. I caught sight of Louisa, our eyes meeting for a second then quickly flitting away.

"And it looks like we have a few new students to SHMS. Why don't we go around and introduce ourselves; tell us what school you transferred from and maybe something fun that you did over the summer."

I could feel the sweat from my bangs drip down the side of my face. What was I going to say? I spent the summer negotiating an embarrassing voice change in front of an entire cast and creative team?

"Let's start with Jack Goodrich. Are you present?"

I snapped to attention.

"Erm—yes," I said, my voice sounding weaker than I'd intended.

"Oh, right in front of my face," Mrs. Lamon murmured, peering down her nose through a pair of thin red-framed glasses. "Would you like to tell us a little about yourself?"

My heart began racing. I hadn't anticipated having to speak on the first day.

"Uh, sure," I said a little louder. "Hi, I'm Jack . . . Good . . . rich." My name suddenly sounded foreign to me, like a bunch of strange syllables mashed together.

"And . . . ?" She squinted. "What school did you go to last year? You're not from Shaker Heights, correct?"

"No-o," my voice squeaked. I was trapped. Announcing to the world that I went to a place called the Professional Performing Arts School would seal my deal as bully bait. "It was called PS 87," I lied, giving the name of my old elementary school.

A snort cut through the classroom, followed by a smattering of giggles from a group of boys sitting nearby.

"Yeah, weird name, I know." I shrugged. "In New York they like to number things instead of name them."

"Wow, New York," Mrs. Lamon said, sitting up in her chair. "That must have been exciting. So . . ." She tilted her head. "What made you move to Ohio?"

As if by stage direction, a clap of thunder rumbled in the distance. I swallowed hard and quickly looked over my shoulder at Louisa. Her eyes widened.

"Um. Well—" I tugged slightly at my collar. "My

dad. My dad got a job here in Cleveland."

"Interesting," Mrs. Lamon said, looking back to her folder. "Does anyone have a question for Mr. Goodrich?"

Questions?! She neglected to mention that my introduction would include a Q&A portion! The room hung silent for a moment until an older-looking boy in an Abercrombie hoodie raised his hand. I cringed, realizing he was from the group of boys who was snickering.

"Yes. Mister—"

"Tanner," he said, crossing his arms and leaning back in his seat.

"What sports did you play at . . . PS . . . Whatever?" he laughed like he'd made the best joke in the world.

I shifted nervously in my seat. Why couldn't I be back in New York? At PPAS it would have been totally acceptable to jump up on my desk and wail a big, "*Whoo-ohh-ohhhh*," condemning my new tormentor like that rocker kid at the end of *Matilda*. But here all I could do was force out an agreeable laugh, attempting to join in on his stupid "joke."

"Tanner," Mrs. Lamon said, shooting him a look to be quiet. I glanced across the room, mortified to realize that everyone was actually waiting for an answer.

"Um," I said, clearing my throat. "You know, just the usual . . . sports," I muttered to the immediate snorting of Tanner and his friends.

"Tanner, I didn't catch your last name?" Mrs. Lamon interrupted.

"Tanner Falzone." He grinned.

"Uh-huh," she said knowingly, flipping through the pages of her leather notebook. "I think I had your older brother, Taylor, was it?"

"Yeah." He smiled slyly.

"Yes, I remember he just *adored* my lesson on *Little Women*," she replied smartly. Even I couldn't help but smile a bit.

"Any other questions for Jack?" she continued. "Yes. The girl in the back with the white headband, you are . . . ?"

"Louisa Benning. But everyone calls me Lou."

I froze in my seat, feeling sweat drip down the inside of my arms. *Well, this is it*, I told myself. *Here goes my cover.* Suddenly the loudspeaker buzzed to life with static. *Saved.*

"ATTENTION, SHMS STUDENTS," a woman's voice screeched. Even a non-actor could tell she'd benefit from moving a few inches away from the mic. "SIGN-UPS for extracurricular activities have JUST. BEEN. POSTED in the lunchroom." My classroom began to vibrate with whispers of conversation.

"*KXSUXUSHUXKSSSSKKHKXKSHHH*," the loudspeaker suddenly hissed, its feedback forcing the entire class to clap their hands over their ears in pain.

"DON'T FORGET TO SIGN UP!" the voice barked.

Even Mrs. Lamon was cringing, gently covering her ear with a single index finger.

"ADDITIONALLY, for your enjoyment, COACH WILSON will be screening a special presentation of last year's soccer championship game during lunch hour. ENJOY YOUR FIRST DAY OF SCHOOL!" The speaker fizzled into silence.

Mrs. Lamon slowly inhaled. "Where was I?"

I kept my head down.

"Oh right," she continued. "New students." She looked down at her leather book. "Do we have a . . . Molly Shaw?"

"Present!" said the perky blond girl sitting next to me, raising her hand.

I spent the morning avoiding all interactions with my classmates, playing an aboveground version of Marco Polo. When we took to the halls to change rooms, I tried to blend in with the other kids, keeping a safe distance from the hoodie-wearing boys and the girl whose secret held my social downfall. As the bell rang at the end of science class, I looked down at my crumpled schedule. "Lunch."

I dashed out of the room and headed to my locker. I peeked inside my brown paper lunch bag—edamame, hummus, carrots sticks, and a fruit leather. Guess mom had discovered the Whole Foods. While I appreciated her effort, a peanut-butter sandwich might have been a little less eye-catching.

Lunch was ordinarily my favorite time of the school day. It was the chance to hang with friends, recap our favorite TV shows, and discuss weekend plans. However, the thought of having to discuss my reason for moving here was enough to wish for five more hours of math. I pushed open the cafeteria doors to the smells of pizza and apple juice. I walked slowly, scanning for a table to sit at. I caught sight of some boys from my class laughing and spooning Jell-O into their mouths. Nope, Tanner was at that table. I walked toward another one, where a group of girls were talking loudly and sipping from juice boxes. Nope, that might send the wrong message. Finally I saw an empty table near the garbage cans, away from the mass of students. Bingo. I reached for a chair when—

"*Jack*," a voice called from behind me. I didn't have to turn around to know who it belonged to.

"Hi, Louisa," I mumbled.

"Do you want to sit with me and my friends?" she said, pointing over to a table of kids from my class.

"Um, I was just gonna sit here."

"Okay, suit yourself." She frowned. "Wait," she piped up. "Can I talk to you for a second?"

"Yeah. Sure," I said, taking a seat.

"So, what was with that introduction in homeroom? You should have told them the real reason you were in New York."

"Oh, that thing I told you last week about being on Broadway?" I grunted. "Yeah, let's forget you ever heard me say that."

She scrunched her eyebrows.

"Look, being the new kid is hard enough when

you're *normal*," I continued. "For now, I just need to try to blend in."

"Are you kidding?" she said, dropping her lunch bag on the table. "You actually have something going for you. Do you know how boring our lives seem compared to yours? I bet everyone would be psyched if they knew the truth."

"Oh sure!" I snapped. "Because *you* gave me the *warmest* of welcomes."

Louisa bit her lower lip. "Look," she said. "I'm sorry for the way I acted last week. I guess I was just in shock or jealous or something. I mean, you have to admit your story was a little crazy, and I'm used to being the only one around here who really cares about theater. Like, other kids do the school plays and stuff, but they wouldn't know a Tony Award from Tony Hawk. So suddenly I'm standing on the sidewalk, and you're busting out Tony-winning choreography, and I'm just supposed to be all, 'Oh cool. Well, I'm Lou!'"

"Actually, *Poppins* was only nominated that year. *Spring Awakening* won for choreography." I couldn't help correcting her.

"Are you sure?" she asked, seeming pretty sure of herself.

"Yeah. *Poppins* won for best choreography when it was still in London, but Bill T. Jones won it over here for that angsty, modern stuff in *Spring Awakening.*"

"*Exactly!*" she shrieked. "Which proves my point. *You're* an MTN! *I'm* an MTN. Let's just put last week behind us and be friends."

"MTN?" I squinted. "Excuse me?"

"Musical Theater Nerd. My friends at Camp Curtain Up came up with it." She smirked.

"Listen," I whispered. "As far as you're concerned, I'm not a Musical Theater anything. You saw how Tanner and those boys acted when they found out I was from New York. What do you think they'd do if they found out I took ballet every week?"

"My friend Jenny takes ballet!" Louisa chimed in.

"Good for her," I replied. "I don't do that anymore. For now I just need to keep quiet, go to class, remember where my locker is, and try not to get stuffed in one, okay?"

She uncrossed her arms. "Okay. Look, if you want me to keep your secret, that's cool, I will. But that doesn't mean you have to act like I don't exist."

I slumped deeper into my chair.

"You know, for someone who had the greatest

job in the world—entertaining people and making them feel happy—you're kind of a downer," she bristled. "No offense."

I knew she was right. I'd spent the past two months sulking around like some kind of Eeyore. It wasn't her fault I got fired and my parents moved me away from New York.

"Sorry," I said finally. "It's not that I don't want to be your friend. It's just you keep talking about how great musicals are, and . . . I guess what I mean to say is"—I felt my throat tightening—"they're not always that *fun* and *magical*."

She looked at me, confused. Her eyes searched my face, as if hoping an appropriate response was printed somewhere on my forehead.

"Suit yourself," she said, picking her lunch off the table. "When you get sick of trying to be like every other lame boy in this school, you know where I live." She turned to go. "And I may have that Sondheim documentary saved on my DVR, just sayin'—"

"JELLLLL-OOOOO BOMB!" a voice cried out.

I turned my head to the sound of wicked laughter erupting from a nearby table. There was Tanner, armed with a bent plastic spoon, and his troop of bros slapping each other's backs. I trailed their jeers to a smallish-looking boy, sitting by himself and glumly wiping red Jell-O off the front of his shirt.

"Thanks for the invite," I mumbled sarcastically to Louisa. "See ya later." I stood up and walked toward the garbage cans, passing Tanner reloading his spoon slingshot, the boy with the Jell-O stain, and a stocky man in a blue tracksuit wheeling a television to the front of the room. I walked to the wall where a dozen sheets of paper, bearing pencil-scrawled names I had never seen, had been taped up. I scanned the lists of activities until I found the one I was looking for. I could feel a set of eyes watching me as I reached into my pocket and pulled out a pencil. I glanced back for a second at Louisa then turned and neatly printed my name, "Jack Goodrich." Soccer tryouts would be next Friday at four o'clock.

Chapter

–LOUISA–

Thump. Thump. Tha-thump. Tha-thump-thump.
Another thing about the universe: It has a wicked
sense of humor. Here it was, my first Saturday
morning since school started, and not only was I
up at 8:30 a.m.—*8:30 a.m.!*—but the reason I was up
was Jack Goodrich. Jack was kicking a soccer ball
against his garage door, over and over and *over*
again. It didn't matter that he lived two houses
down from us. The unfortunate position of my
bedroom window made it seem as though he was
kicking the ball inside my room. *Tha-thump.* I lay in
bed waiting for one of his parents—heck, *anyone*—
to tell him to stop—that maybe he should pursue

a quieter hobby, like chess, or scuba diving. That he was disturbing the neighbors—*one neighbor in particular*. But I was not to be satisfied; no one said a word. Apparently I was the only one in our subdivision who liked to sleep in on weekends.

Truthfully, I was less troubled about not getting my ten hours of uninterrupted slumber than I was about Jack's behavior during the past week. While I no longer felt as if I needed to avoid him (thankfully, since we had the same class schedule), I also felt like I couldn't really talk to him (since he had chosen to deny everything about himself). Our cafeteria conversation on the first day of school was the last exchange we'd had, punctuated in not-so-subtle fashion by his signing up for soccer-team tryouts.

After that, I'd spent the rest of the week watching him impressively dodge questions from our other classmates. Tanner asked him what kind of music he listened to, and he said Green Day and Duncan Sheik. *I* knew that was code for *American Idiot* (a musical adapted from Green Day's concept album) and *Spring Awakening* (score by Duncan Sheik), but obviously Tanner wasn't going to make that connection. All he'd said was "Green Day?

That's so old school." Jack had replied, "I guess," then sighed with what I perceived to be relief as Tanner turned his attention to hassling Isabelle Montstream for Sour Patch Kids.

Of course I couldn't observe Jack without Jenny noticing.

She had happily mistaken my Jack-fixation for love, and proceeded to have a little too much fun teasing me about my "new crush."

"'I mean, he *is* cute, but that is completely different from me *thinking* he's cute,'" she'd whispered to me during science class on Wednesday, quoting what I'd said weeks earlier in the privacy of her bedroom.

"Shhh!" I'd hissed.

"She's a small-town girl; he's from the big city," she cooed breathlessly. *"Will they overcome their differences and find true love in each other's arms?"*

Jenny liked to turn unremarkable moments into commercials for made-for-TV movies. Most of the time, they made me laugh. When they were about my love life, they made me squirm.

"Gross! Stop it!"

Admittedly, I *had* been staring at Jack a little too long, but it had nothing to do with love. I knew there was more to his story than he was letting on, thanks to a productive Google search I'd made the night before: "Jack Goodrich Broadway." While the links I'd clicked on didn't fill in all the details, I'd unearthed enough information about him to suspect that being the new kid wasn't the only thing making his transition into Shaker Heights difficult. But because he had practically begged me not to talk about his life in New York, I didn't know how to approach him.

Whatever. Jack's unrelenting soccer practice at eight thirty on a Saturday morning made me feel a lot less curious, and certainly less sympathetic toward him. That stupid soccer ball! And its repetitive *thump-thump-tha-thump* against his garage door! I rolled over in bed and reached for my iPod then scrolled until I found "Forget About the Boy" from *Thoroughly Modern Millie* and channeled my frustration through the lyrics:

"Pull the plug,
Ain't he the one
Who pulled the rug?"

I must have been singing along louder than I thought because all of a sudden I heard my mom calling from downstairs.

"Lou? Are you *up*?"

"Sort of."

"Wow. It's early for you," she called, stating the obvious.

"I *know*."

"Well, come down to the kitchen when you're *up* up. There's something I think you should see."

Dad was sitting at the kitchen counter holding the Arts section of *Sun Press* as I shuffled in, a small smile curling the edges of his mouth. Mom had a similar look as she poured herself a cup of coffee.

"What should I see?" I asked.

Dad handed me the Arts section, folded back on itself to reveal a story about the expansion of a local pottery studio, movie times, an advertisement for ballroom dancing classes . . . and an announcement for the Shaker Heights Community Players production of *Into the Woods*. I looked at my parents.

"I thought . . . I thought they were doing *Chess*," I stammered.

"Looks like there's been a change of plans," Mom said, sipping her coffee. I looked back at the newspaper ad in disbelief. Auditions were going to be held on September fifteenth. Six days from now. Rehearsals would start September twentieth. Opening night: November first. I think I stopped breathing for a few seconds.

"You okay, Lou?" my dad asked.

I took a gulp of air.

"Do you think I have a chance?" I whispered.

"Why not?" Mom said, reaching into the pantry for a box of pancake mix. "I'm sure you know that part better than anyone in town."

"But Little Red is usually played by a grown-up," I said, suddenly doubtful.

"So go prove to them that she can be played by a real kid," urged Dad. "Leave Cinderella and Rapunzel and the rest of the parts to the adults."

"Doug, I'm so proud of you!" Mom gushed. "You've been paying attention!"

"Well, Hannah, when one is forced to listen to *Into the Woods* as much as I am, one can't help but retain—"

"Still, honey, I'm impressed . . ."

"Glad I can still impress you after all these years . . ."

Their words overlapped and fell away as I pictured myself in a cape and holding a basket, skipping across a stage and delivering lines with a perfect blend of pluckiness and sarcasm.

I felt tingly. Here was a chance—a real chance at living a dream. A calendar of the week leading up to Friday's audition began to map itself out in my mind. Today would be all about familiarizing myself with Little Red's songs (like I didn't know them by heart, but still—I wasn't going to take *anything* for granted). Tomorrow I would try to squeeze in an appointment with my voice teacher, Maureen, who would help me identify the right places in the music to breathe, as well as the best way to support my sound while also making sure my diction was sharp.

According to the newspaper ad, the audition sides were already posted on the Players' website, so on Monday I would start working on Little Red's scenes with Jenny, who always liked to help me prepare. She had terrible stage fright when it came to speaking in front of people, but alone with me, she was a real ham. I could already hear her reading the part of the Wolf. Tuesday through Thursday would be a repeat of Saturday through Monday. I was an unstoppable force; the role would be *mine*. Total *Into the Woods* immersion would begin in three . . . two . . .

THA-THUMP! I was snapped out of my concentration. Had that stupid soccer ball gotten *heavier*?

And suddenly, just as clearly as I'd pictured myself wearing a red cape, I now pictured Jack—my Broadway-star-in-hiding-neighbor Jack—holding magic beans, growing a beanstalk, and singing about giants in the sky. *Ugh*. He would be *perfect* as Jack, their shared name a mere coincidence. But destiny was being challenged by a soccer ball. And I was instantly annoyed.

"Why the frown?" Mom asked, once again reminding me that I had the worst poker face.

Why the frown? *Tha-THUMP*. That's why.

"Uh . . . Nothing. This is great. I'm going to practice all weekend." I grabbed the Arts section, turned from the kitchen counter, and started marching down the hallway toward the front door, a conversation forming in my head.

"Should I just put the *Into the Woods* soundtrack on a loop?" Dad joked.

"It's a *cast recording*, and *yes*," I said, sliding on my flip-flops and opening the door.

"Where are you going? I'm making magic get-the-part pancakes!" Mom called after me.

"I'll be back in a couple minutes. I just have to talk to Jack."

"*Who's Jack?*"

"Our neighbor!" I called over my shoulder. As I stepped off our front stoop, I heard Mom say to Dad, slightly bewildered, "I didn't realize she'd met him." It was probably time to fill them in. Right now, however, I had something that demanded immediate attention.

Jack's hair was plastered to his forehead; he was a sweaty mess. From his driveway, he saw me approaching, and rather than pick up the soccer ball and say hello, he kicked it into the garage door extra hard, as if to make a point. *Tha-thump.*

I waved the newspaper in the air.

"Did you see this?" I called to him, my flip-flops sliding on the wet grass. This neighborhood was fanatical about their sprinklers.

Jack squinted at me. "What is it?"

His delivery of the question was so casual that I was instantly suspicious.

"Are you pretending not to know, or do you really not know?" What had gotten into me? I was feeling so feisty.

As I stepped onto his driveway, Jack finally stopped the soccer ball with his foot and sighed, exasperated. "*Into the Woods*?"

"Ha-*ha*!" I exclaimed. "I knew you'd seen it."

"So what? It's not like I'm going to audition for it."

Jack rolled the soccer ball over the top of his foot and flicked it toward his chest, bumping it back into his hands. Unimpressed, I continued my campaign.

"C'mon, why not? You don't want to play Jack? It's an amazing role!"

Jack's nostrils flared, defiant.

"*No.* I don't."

"You know you'd get the part. Once they see *Broadway* on your résumé, you probably won't even have to audition." (That last part wasn't true, but I was certain he'd get cast—Amy Judd had grown out her hair and gained about fifteen pounds since playing Winthrop last year.)

"I don't care," Jack said.

"Tell me you don't want to sing 'Giants in the Sky.'"

At the mention of the song, I thought I saw a hint of interest flicker across Jack's face, but then he scrunched up his mouth and inhaled sharply through his nose.

"I don't want to sing 'Giants in the Sky.'"

"It's a really great song."

Jack dropped the soccer ball, stopped it with his foot, and looked me squarely in the eye.

"Louisa, nothing you say is going to change my mind. I have no interest in auditioning for *Into the Woods*."

I stared back at him, equally stubborn.

"I don't believe you," I said. I had never been so courageous in a conversation.

"What do you mean, you *don't believe me*?" Jack said, smirking. "You hardly know me."

Without thinking, I blurted out, "I know you were supposed to play the lead in *The Big Apple*. You should be rehearsing for it in New York right now."

Tha-thump. You would have thought I'd kicked the soccer ball directly into Jack's chest. His face went pale. I sensed immediately that I had said a terrible thing.

"Sorry," I murmured. I had not meant to be hurtful. Unsure of what to say next, I looked down at the driveway, as if I might find the right words written across its surface. All I saw was an expanse of licorice-black asphalt glaring angrily in the hot sun.

"It's just . . . I looked you up online," I said, hastily, "because you were . . . You didn't want to talk about your life in New York . . . and I was curious, so . . . Sorry."

I looked up to see Jack's eyes glistening. Were those *tears*?

What kind of monster was I?

Clearly the kind of monster who was really good at destroying chances for friendship. The Arts section of *Sun Press* felt like a dumbbell in my hand, heavy with shame.

It seemed like an eternity before Jack spoke.

"If you knew the reason why I'm not in rehearsals for *The Big Apple*," he said carefully, his jaw tight, "then you would know why I can't—why I'm *not* going to audition for *Into the Woods*."

He picked up the soccer ball once more and stared at me in a way that I knew the conversation was over.

One thing about being an actor: You have to know when it's your cue to exit the scene.

"Okay, never mind," I said, wondering how I could ever repair the apparent damage I'd done. "Sorry to bother you."

I turned and walked back to my house, hating myself not only for upsetting him, but for being more curious about Jack Goodrich than ever.

Chapter

Nine

-JACK-

It was mid-July and the end of our first week of rehearsals for *The Big Apple*. The cast had gathered in the large studio to read through the entire show. In addition to the creative team, two rows of chairs had been assembled for the producers— suit-wearing men and high-heeled ladies, chatting and checking their cell phones. The yakking began to subside as a melody tinkled on the piano. The musical began with my character singing in a spotlight, a single voice cutting through the babbling of a crowded subway platform. Our music director nodded. I took a deep breath and began.

"One song. One song worth singing. One voice, like

a bell that needs ringing." The room was quiet as a museum, all eyes staring directly at me.

"One song, and I sing it for youuuuu." My throat tightened as the note came out strained. *"One song,"* I soldiered on, *"all you need to break through."*

As the show continued, I only got worse. Passages that had never tripped me up suddenly twisted in my throat. I struggled to hit my high notes and could feel my voice getting weaker with every number. As the finale came to a close, I could tell there was a shift in the room. The producers began chatting, this time in low whispers. The director huddled next to the composer and lyricist and pointed aggressively to places in the score. Worst of all, my cast, *my new family,* who just days earlier talked and laughed with me on breaks, now avoided my eye contact, quickly packing up their rehearsal bags and hurrying out of the room.

Much had changed at Shaker Heights Middle School since my run-in with Louisa in front of my garage. I no longer had to worry about her blabbing my secret to the entire school. In fact, her whole demeanor seemed to have changed overnight. Her feistiness and sarcasm turned into sympathy; she became almost apologetic with every little interaction we had. I'd finally gotten what I'd been praying for—someone to feel as sorry for me as I had been feeling for myself. It was incredibly sweet. It was also driving me insane.

When I took a seat in homeroom, I spied her from across the room giving me an encouraging smile and a thumbs-up. *What for?* I wondered. *Remembering where my assigned seat is?* In science I caught her gazing at me during Mr. Buckshaw's lecture on magnets, a sad look on her face. In Spanish class she sat two chairs in front of me. When Señora DeGuzman asked the class "*¿Cómo se dice* . . . an apple?*" Louisa immediately snapped her head back, her wide eyes seeming to apologize on Señora's behalf for bringing up anything *Big Apple* related. *You must be joking,* I thought, raising my hand.

"Señor Goodrich."

"*Manzana*," I answered, rolling my eyes.

After class I decided to nab her in the hallway.

"Louisa, we gotta talk."

"Is this about what happened in music class when Mrs. Wagner brought up *singing,* because my heart went out to you. *Too soon*, I know, but she didn't know that you're in a delicate place right n—"

"No, look," I cut her off forcefully. "I know you're being sensitive and feeling sorry for me, and that's awesome, but I'll be honest, it's driving me crazy."

"Oh." She looked slightly offended.

"Look, here's the story." I paused, deciding to be totally straight with her. "I got fired from that show *The Big Apple*. My voice started changing, and it was really embarrassing."

"Omigosh, Jack," Louisa said softly, her eyes becoming glassy.

"Yeah, no, I mean, it's fine." I suddenly felt like *I* was the one who needed to do the comforting. "I'm okay," I said, brushing it off. "It's just, I'm not really looking for a pity party or anything."

"Okay, yeah, I totally understand. I'm so sorry."

"No. It's cool."

We stood there for a moment. The sound of slamming lockers filled a very long, uncomfortable pause.

"You know what you need to do, Jack?" she said, suddenly seized with excitement. "What would make you feel better? You need to audition for *Into the Woods*!"

"No, Louisa. That's not a good idea—"

"Yes! The best thing you can do is get back on the horse!" she said, grabbing my arm.

"*No, Louisa.* I told you, it's not gonna happen. Besides, soccer tryouts are the same day, and I really want to make the team."

A bell rang, signaling we were late for class.

"Okay, whatever," she said, slinging her backpack over her shoulder and whizzing past me. "Hurry up, slowpoke, we're going to be late."

As I chased her down the hallway, I grew thankful that Louisa's bleeding-heart friend act was over, but as the school day continued, I realized I'd ignored the very first lesson of *Into the Woods*: "Be careful what you wish for."

It started in the computer lab. Our teacher, Ms. Stark, was leading the class in a typing lesson.

"You have ten minutes to finish your exercise," Ms. Stark said, plopping down at her desk.

Piece of cake, I thought, swiftly tapping away at the keys like a concert pianist. Even though I was only twelve, I considered myself pretty computer savvy. In the past month I'd redesigned my mom's

food blog, *Tale as Old as Thyme,* and scanned my
dad's vintage map collection to his hard drive.
Finishing my lesson early, I slyly shifted my gaze
to Ms. Stark, who at the moment seemed occupied,
uncoiling a tangled mess of cords. I discreetly
minimized the typing screen and clicked on a web
browser. As my email page loaded, I immediately
noticed a new message from someone named
LegallyMTN@me.com with a link and two words:
"for you."

I clicked on the link. "There Are Giants in
the Sky!" blasted from my computer, causing me
to jump in my seat. I began fake coughing and
scrambling to *x* out of the window just as Ms. Stark
peeked up from her wire nest. "You all right, Jack?"

"Yeah, fine," I wheezed. "Allergies." I patted my
chest with my fist. The video I'd opened must have
been from the Broadway-recorded video of *Into the
Woods.* There was only one person this could have
come from . . . I looked across the room at Louisa.
She sat hunched over, banging on her keyboard,
seemingly oblivious to the eruption of Sondheim.

Tuesday brought another surprise, this time in
math class. Early in the hour I excused myself to go
to the bathroom. When I got back, our teacher, Mr.

Breslin, asked us to open our textbooks to Chapter 3: Percentages. I unzipped my backpack and found a strange binder I'd never seen before. I pulled it out, flipped open the cover, and immediately rolled my eyes. The first page read clearly, *INTO THE WOODS: Libretto* (which is just a fancy word meaning *script*). I looked over my shoulder at Louisa, sitting two rows behind me. Head dropped, she was scrutinizing a math problem. Refusing to give her the satisfaction of a successful heist, I slipped the script back into my bag.

The hint-dropping continued for the rest of the week. Wednesday was met with a downpour of Facebook messages and wall posts containing pictures and articles about Stephen Sondheim. Thursday, my locker had been crammed with little pieces of paper, each bearing a different quote from the show. While I was pretty sure this girl was clinically insane, I couldn't help but be a *little* impressed by her enthusiasm and knowledge of theater.

Finally, it was the day of soccer tryouts. It was also the day of the *Into the Woods* auditions. Soon enough I'd be a part of a club, and Louisa would have no choice but to give up her crusade. I opened my locker cautiously, half expecting tree branches to fall out. Nothing. I walked into homeroom and immediately checked under my desk. No audition flyers or sheet music. As the day progressed, I began wondering if Louisa had actually called it quits. Without the anticipation of her next move, morning classes seemed to drag on forever. Finally the lunch bell rang, and I hurried to the cafeteria. I pushed through the doorway with the other kids but was intercepted.

"*Jack, Jack, Jack. Head in a sack,*" Louisa said, leaping up from a nearby lunch table.

"What is it now?" I said, crossing my arms, secretly amused. "Do you have some magic beans you plan on sneaking into my lunch bag or something?"

"I do not." She frowned. "They were sold out at the Stop & Shop, but I *am* glad you've noticed. For a while, I was beginning to think you hadn't been getting my little messages."

"How could I have missed your messages? You wrote in chalk on our driveway: *Check your Facebook!*"

"Yeah, that may have been too much."

"Well, spill it," I demanded. "I need to go talk

to the guys and see what to expect at tryouts this evening."

"You're seriously still going through with the soccer tryouts?" She groaned. "Jack, you're not like them."

"Wow, thanks for the encouragement—"

"No, I mean, *you're not like them*. You're special," she said, tilting her head. "You got cast in a Broadway show! What are the chances of that, like, one in a million? A lot of people must have really believed in you. You're seriously going to trade that to be just another jersey on a field?"

I opened my mouth to respond, but she cut me off. "Look. I know you said you want to see if there's something else that will make you happy, but do you really think it's going to come from lying about who you really are?" She was relentless. "If you're looking for a group of people who are *actually* cool and will understand you and aren't going to judge you for nerding out about rare cast albums or shaky bootlegs of *Rent*, you're not gonna find them on the field. You're going to find them with the Players.

"Here," she said, handing me a packet of paper. "It's the audition scene. I already highlighted your lines, and I printed off directions for your parents." I took the papers from her. She'd highlighted my lines in green.

I could tell she was a desperate. "Well, thanks, I guess . . . ," I said, looking down at the sides. A wave of nerves and excitement rumbled in my stomach, just like it always did before an audition or first rehearsal. The last time I felt it was in July, meeting my cast for the first time and feeling (stupidly) like I was a member of a new family.

"But there's another reason I can't audition for your show," I said, swallowing hard. "I don't think I want to perform anymore."

A look of total disappointment washed over her face.

"Getting fired from a show kinda put things in perspective, if you know what I mean. Like, when I first started doing musicals it was all about playing and having fun, but during *The Big Apple* I was suddenly scared to go to work. I'd stay up all night staring at the ceiling, wondering if tomorrow would be the day they'd tell me not to come back." As the words came out of my mouth, I realized these were things I'd never shared with anyone. "Sometimes it doesn't matter how much time you've spent learning your lines or how hard you're trying to make everyone like you. If your best isn't good enough, they can always find someone to replace you."

Louisa stood there in stunned silence.

"And honestly, I don't even know if I can sing anymore," I mumbled. "So while I appreciate all your enthusiasm and everything, I just want . . . I *need* to find something else I'm good at."

I looked into her eyes. Her face bore a familiar look. It was the same one I'd gotten when I told her I was in *Mary Poppins* and then again when I performed the letters in "Supercal."

"Okay," she said finally. "I'm sorry. That sucks."

"Yeah." I shrugged.

"Well, at least do me a favor."

Oh no, I thought, bracing for a ridiculous request.

"At soccer tryouts," she mumbled, "try to kick some butt."

The rest of the day flew by. Before I knew it, I was cramming my textbooks into my locker and grabbing my duffel bag packed with soccer shorts, a jersey, a set of shiny white shin guards, and a pair of black cleats. It felt weird staying at school while the rest of the kids were hopping on the bus or piling in with their car pools. The parking lot had pretty much emptied out by the time I walked from the back entrance to the soccer field. As I got closer, I spied a dark green minivan parked by the fence with unmistakable New York State plates. I approached the car and knocked gently on the driver's window.

"Dad, what are you doing here?" I said through the glass.

"Oh hey, Jack Sprat!" my dad said, enthusiastically rolling down his window.

"You know the tryouts aren't over till five thirty, right?"

"Yeah, I know." He nodded. "But your mom said that she might have forgotten to pack your water bottle, so I drove over to bring you one just in case."

I looked down at my duffel bag, the outline of a bottle clearly visible against the nylon fabric.

"Nope, she definitely packed it." I smiled.

"Huh." My dad shrugged. "Well, just in case

you need a second one I've got it in the back." He began fidgeting with his seatbelt. "I know how sometimes you get thirsty and—"

"Dad," I cut him off. "It's okay if you just wanted to come and watch."

"Oh!" he said after a short silence. "Well, that might be nice. But I know you sometimes get weird about performing in front of us, so if it's all right with you, I can just watch from the car."

"Sure, Dad." I smiled. "That would be fine."

I looked over to the field, where a man was making his way to the guys trying out for soccer. I recognized him as Coach Wilson, the man in the tracksuit pushing the projector in the cafeteria on the first day of school.

"Okay, I should probably go," I said. "I'll see you at five thirty."

"Break a leg, Jack Sprat!" my dad called as I jogged toward the field.

The closer I got, the bigger and scarier the guys seemed to appear. They were stretching and lacing up their cleats with grunts and growls of effortless masculinity. *Break a leg*, I repeated in my head. That expression never seemed like a threat until now.

We began with a set of drills. One by one, Coach Wilson had us dribble a ball to an orange cone, circle it, and run back. I watched as other boys completed the drill with varying degrees of skill. My first attempt was a little clunky. I accidentally kicked the ball too hard and had to chase after it before turning around and bringing it back.

Coach Wilson then split us into two groups: half took turns shooting, the other half acted as goalies, trying to block. I delivered a solid kick, but it sailed right into the arms of Garett, a kid from my homeroom.

Next came my turn as goalie. I uttered a sigh of relief as a kid approached the ball. He was the smallest guy on the field. I recognized him as the boy on the receiving end of Tanner's Jell-O bomb. I spread my feet and put my hands in front of my chest like I'd seen the other boys do. Like a flash, his ball whipped straight past me and into the upper right-hand corner of the net. Judging by the faces of the others, they were just as surprised as I was.

"All right, let's do sprints now," Coach Wilson announced. "I want you to run as fast as you can from one end of the field to the other. I'll be timing you."

Come on, Jack, you got this, I said to myself, shaking out my legs. I knew if I kept sucking, my chance at a normal middle-school life was back to zero. We stood single file, waiting for Coach Wilson's call.

"Yer mark. Get set. *Go!*"

"Yer mark. Get set. *Go!*"

"Yer mark. Get set. *Go!*"

Before I knew it, I was next. Coach Wilson gave me the final *Go!* and I launched into a dash for my life. I flew down the field taking long, controlled strides (guess my ballet training was paying off). I charged with a force I didn't even know I had. With every heaving breath, the doubts I'd been swallowing seemed to release themselves into the crisp September air. I neared the chalk line, confident I'd done all I could do. Two more steps and "*OOoffff!*"

My knees clipped the grass as my body was thrown off balance and tumbled to the ground. I felt my face smash against the cold earth. I blinked open my eyes. A crowd of boys stood frozen, hands like visors over their brows, staring at me.

"You okay, son?" Coach Wilson called, jogging my way.

"Yeah, yeah," I said, clumsily getting back on my feet. I looked down at my shirt, a giant grass stain across my chest. I was totally embarrassed. "I'm sorry," I mumbled to him. If my sucky performance in the drills hadn't sealed the deal, this was certainly the final nail in the coffin.

"What are you sorry about?" he said, smiling. "Do you know how many times you're gonna get knocked down in this game?" He brushed a clod of dirt from my shoulder. *"It's the getting up that's important."*

I hesitated for a moment, considering what he'd just said, then jogged back with him to the group. "Even with your fall," he said, looking back at me, "that was the fastest time today.

"All right." Coach Wilson clapped as he neared the bleachers. "The last thing we're doing is a scrimmage. Bowen through Jasperson, red team. Johnson through Trumble, you guys are blue. Grab a pinnie," he said, pointing to an overflowing laundry bag. I joined the huddle of boys reaching into the heap and pulling out a blue or red mesh jersey, Coach's words still ringing in my head.

"Mr. Wilson?" I asked, glancing over at our green minivan. "Can I run to my car? I think I left my water bottle in there."

Chapter

-LOUISA-

There it was—that twisted-mop feeling in my gut. I had never felt it quite as strongly as I did upon entering the lobby of Shaker Heights High on Friday afternoon, where it seemed like the entire town had come to audition for the Players' production of *Into the Woods*. It was a madhouse— grown-ups, children . . . even a dog was there (though I didn't exactly know why—maybe that Labrador was auditioning for the Wolf?). There were pairs of people reading scenes by the vending machines, people signing in at a table by the trophy cases, people windmilling their arms and rolling their heads from side to side by the main office. I didn't remember the auditions for *The Music Man* being this crazy.

"Were the auditions for *The Music Man* this crazy?" asked a familiar voice behind me, clearly reading my mind. I turned to see the closest thing to a celebrity the Players had: Denise Zook. Tall and imposing, she wore an eggplant-colored wrap dress and dark-chocolate knee-high boots. She scanned the room with her ice-blue eyes like she owned the place.

"Hi, Denise," I murmured, feeling very small. Even though we had acted opposite each other only a year ago, I was still totally intimidated by her.

"Do you know if the girls' locker room is open?" she asked.

"I don't, sorry."

"I like to do my vocal warm-up in one of the shower stalls. Good acoustics, you know?"

"Sure."

I got the sense she was talking *at* me, not *to* me.

"I'll check with Barry," she said assertively. "He'll let me in even if they're off-limits to everybody else."

I had no idea who Barry was, but that hardly mattered. She would find him and get what she wanted; that's what it meant to be Denise Zook.

"Bet you're glad they decided not to do *Chess*" were Denise's parting words as she strode off, confident, beautiful, and terrifying. At this point, auditioning for the Players was just a formality for her. Everyone knew she'd be cast as the Witch in *Into the Woods*, just like everyone had known she'd be cast as Marion in *The Music Man*, Reno Sweeney in *Anything Goes*, Sally Bowles in *Cabaret* . . . She was really good, and no one believed that more than she did.

I found myself wishing for an ounce of that trademark Zook confidence as I spotted a girl about my age, her face framed by golden ringlets. She was arranging a red-and-white-checkered napkin across a perfect-looking wicker basket, making it clear she was a contender for Little Red Riding Hood. *Props*—why hadn't I thought of that? I nervously touched the ends of my French braids, which Mom had crisscrossed with precision then sprayed solidly into place.

On the ride here, I had felt buzzy with excitement. Now I just felt overwhelmed.

It didn't matter that my audition sides were in perfect order or that my lines were highlighted

in green (green for trees, trees are in the *woods*).
It didn't matter that I knew Little Red's song, "I
Know Things Now," backward and forward, that
I'd practically been singing it in my sleep for the
last week. It didn't matter that Jenny had read my
scenes with me so many times that she almost
knew the lines better than I did. And it certainly
didn't matter that I wanted the part more than
anything I'd ever wanted in my life—because there
was a chance that's how all of the other girls felt,
too. The only thing that mattered was the audition
itself. All the dreaming and preparation wouldn't
mean much if I didn't succeed when it counted.

"Lou?" My dad's voice surprised me. I'd forgotten
that he'd been parking the car. My parents and I
had agreed that it was better for Dad to accompany
me to the auditions, even if it meant him having
to leave work early. Mom tended to get as nervous
in these kinds of situations as I did, while Dad
managed to remain cool.

"You having thought flurries?" he asked,
tucking his keys into his pocket.

"Yeah," I admitted, allowing myself to smile at
his observation.

Dad had coined that phrase a few years back,

in response to the way I froze at the entrance of Cedar Point, this huge amusement park on Lake Erie. I was so overwhelmed by the number of roller coasters and other rides that I couldn't speak. That's when Dad said it looked like my brain was caught in a little storm—"thought flurries"—and it seemed like such a perfect description that the phrase had stuck.

"What's going on?" Dad asked, placing a reassuring hand on top of my head.

"I'm wondering if I should have brought a picnic basket," I said, eyeing Miss Props-i-Locks with concern.

"Do you want one? I can run home and grab ours from the basement," Dad offered.

I considered taking him up on it when I suddenly flashed back to camp, where Avery, my favorite acting instructor, had stressed the importance of "trusting your preparation."

"It's natural to doubt yourself in an audition environment," she'd said. "You enter a waiting room and immediately see people who are *like* you, but maybe a little bit taller, maybe a little prettier, a little younger. But none of them *are* you. And if *you're* the one who's supposed to get the part, then why sabotage yourself by changing something at the last minute? *Trust* the work you've done, and your talent—and most of all, your uniqueness—will shine through."

Thank you, Avery, I thought, silently dismissing Props-i-Locks.

"No, it's okay, Dad," I said decisively, "it would only distract me."

"All right, then," he said. "Why don't we get you signed in?"

We crossed the lobby to the table by the trophy cases, where an overly friendly woman wearing a name tag announcing "Hello My Name Is **GINA!**" asked me for my name. As I spelled *Benning*, I glanced up to see a huge trophy in the case behind her boasting a Shaker Heights High Soccer Champions label. And of course I pictured Jack, who must have been at this very moment running back and forth on our school's playing field, burying the memories of his theater life with each kick, each . . . shuffle? (Listen, if I knew proper soccer terminology, I probably wouldn't have been handing my head shot and résumé to "Hello My Name Is **GINA!**")

I uttered a small sigh as I thought of my failed

attempts at convincing Jack to audition with me. At least he'd had a sense of humor about my antics. While he might not have become my new best friend, he hadn't become my new worst enemy, either. Still, I wished he were there. As I left **GINA!** to fill out a personal-information form, I saw only a handful of boys who looked like they were there to audition for the role of Jack. A couple of them looked downright miserable—one had clearly been dragged there by his mother, who if I were to guess by her excessive makeup, costume jewelry, and hoop skirt, was there to audition for Cinderella's Stepmother. Another boy couldn't stop hiccuping.

"Lou? Did you grab a pen?" Dad asked, leading the way toward a bench.

"Uh, I forgot," I said, my eyes darting back and forth across the lobby. It seemed like the number of people had *doubled* since our arrival. My breathing became shallow as my twisted mop got—*twistier.*

"You okay there, Lou?"

"Mm-hmm."

"I'm wondering if your thought flurries might have just become a blizzard." Dad chuckled, reaching for a pen from his inside jacket pocket.

"It's just . . . ," I began, taking a seat on the bench, "this is intense."

Dad smiled.

"And exciting."

He sat next to me while I filled out my form.

"How long till you're up?" he asked casually.

"They're seeing Little Reds at five forty-five," I said, looking at the clock above the lobby doors. "So in, like, fifteen minutes."

I had already warmed up at home, but the thought of just sitting still for fifteen minutes in the middle of this chaos, where you could practically smell the desperation, made me extra tense. Dad, sensing my agitation, made a suggestion.

"Why don't you take a walk? Don't worry about me. I can watch the Reds game," he said, holding up his phone, "or should I say the *Little Reds* game?" He winked at me, proud of his joke.

"Yeah, okay." I laughed and got up from our bench.

The auditions were being held in the auditorium to the left of the lobby, so I walked to the right, toward the gymnasium, where it was quieter. I turned down an empty hallway, where rows of lockers and a humming water fountain greeted me with complete disinterest. I felt better immediately. I could hear my own breathing begin to slow and deepen. Props-i-Locks, Denise, **GINA!**, and the Labrador all melted away as I closed my eyes and summoned the lyrics of the opening number of *Into the Woods*. They expressed perfectly what I was feeling:

> *"I wish*
> *More than anything*
> *More than life*
> *More than jewels*
> *I wish..."*

They reminded me why I was here and what I wanted to do when it was finally my turn.

After about ten minutes of focused concentration, I was ready to reenter the fray. As I headed back toward the lobby, I stopped in front of the water fountain for a quick drink. Bending down to take a sip, I heard strange-sounding footsteps turning the corner down the hallway: *clack, clack, clack.* And in an instant I knew it was him, even before I stood up and saw with my own eyes that I was right.

He was still in his soccer clothes, still out of breath, holding black dress shoes with a pair of gray pants and a button-down shirt draped over his bare arm. Grass and mud stains blotched his knees, and his soccer cleats made him appear wobbly on the concrete floors. In his other hand he held the sides I'd printed out for him, highlighted in green.

"Hey," Jack said, panting.

(The last thing I wanted was to ruin this movie-perfect moment by saying something that would scare him away, so I just said "Hey" back.)

"Have you auditioned yet?" he asked, half gasping. I wondered whether he had run directly from our soccer field to the high school.

"I'm about to," I said, "in just a few minutes."

Jack nodded but didn't speak. I touched the ends of my braids.

"I was about to make the team, I think," he finally said.

"Yeah?"

"Yeah. But then . . ." He paused. Even though I was more than twenty feet away from him, I could tell he was unsure about the choice he'd just made. He looked like he might bolt at any second, so I needed to proceed with caution.

"Listen," I said, choosing my words carefully. "You've got as good a shot as anyone here, Jack. And no matter what happens, I promise I won't tell anyone. Only if you want me to."

I could see Jack absorbing what I'd just said, his shoulders lowering slightly.

"Okay," he said, nodding tentatively. "Cool." He wiped his forehead with the back of his hand that held the audition sides, and I noticed he'd scribbled some notes in the margins. Like someone who cares would do.

"Do you know where the boys' room is? I need to clean myself up."

I pointed behind me.

"Keep walking; it's on your left."

Jack walked toward me and stopped when we were shoulder to shoulder.

"Thanks, Lou," he said. It was barely a whisper, but I still felt my cheeks get hot because he'd finally called me Lou.

"You're welcome. You're gonna be great."

I hesitated for a second, then squeezed his elbow and resumed my walk back to the lobby.

As I got closer, I could hear **GINA!** announcing,

"If you are here to audition for Little Red Riding Hood, *please* line up to the *left* of the auditorium doors. I will be collecting your information sheets *before* you go in. Thank you!"

Suddenly Jack's voice bounced off the metal lockers with a zing.

"Wait! Lou!"

I turned around.

"Break a leg, okay?" Jack was smiling, and I realized I'd never seen him do that before. It was sort of dazzling, and I saw instantly the Broadway star he was meant to be.

"Thanks!" I called back, grinning like an idiot. "I will."

I hadn't had that many auditions in my life—a handful, really—but I'd had enough to know what a good one felt like. As soon as I set foot on the stage inside the auditorium, it was like something magical happened to me. The twisted mop untwisted. I felt lighter and stronger. I felt like a track runner who knows that no one is going to pass her on the last stretch before the finish line. And I felt like everyone in the auditorium leaned toward me, and I leaned toward them, and then everything that I wanted to say and sing burst out of me like a summer storm.

Chapter

Eleven

–JACK–

The voice hit me like a warm wave. Chills ran up and down my arms as I peeked around the corner in the back of the auditorium.

I had been in the hallway, nervously trying to block out the waiting-room chatter when I heard it. It was the faint hum of something extraordinary. The voice was unmistakable; even through twelve inches of concrete and the solid fact that I'd never heard her sing, I knew it was Lou. I broke away from my crouched huddle by the trophy case and peeked my head stealthily through a door in the back of the theater.

Her tiny frame looked even tinier on the empty

stage, but her voice filled the entire theater. She negotiated the tricky octave leaps and crunchy melodies as if they had lived in her bones for years. During her acting scenes the creative team howled with laughter, particularly her deadpan delivery of the line to Cinderella, "... *You talk to birds?*"

Everything began to make sense: her crazed knowledge of theater, her obsession with auditioning, her need to connect with me about all things New York. She wasn't just someone who loved Broadway. She was a girl designed to be a part of it. *Okay*, I thought, *now I really need to be in this show.*

"Jack Goodrich," a woman's voice called from the hallway. "You're on deck."

She led me through a door that opened to the wings of a backstage. My heart began to race as reality set in. I was about to do the one thing I'd promised to never do again. I was about to gamble with the last bit of confidence I had left, knowing full well that the sting of rejection might be waiting on the other side.

"Hello, Jack," a soothing voice said from the row of tables assembled in the audience. "I don't think we've met before. I'm Renee Florkowski, the director of *Into the Woods*."

"Nice to meet you," I said warmly, stuffing my hands in my pockets to hide their slight tremble.

"So, you're auditioning for Jack, I presume?"

"Yeah." I smiled. "I heard I already missed the time slot for Cinderella's mother, so I figured this would be the next best thing."

Everyone behind the table began to chuckle, putting me, at least momentarily, at ease.

"So, let's start with the scene and then we can go straight into 'Giants in the Sky,'" Renee said. "Maddy is going to be reading with you." She gestured toward the woman walking up the stairs to the stage.

"Sounds great," I replied, looking to Maddy.

"Whenever you're ready," Renee said.

I took a deep breath and gave Maddy a little nod. I gazed at her face trying to imagine that this adult woman was in fact a twelve-year-old with a red cape. She looked down at her script and then back to me, eyebrows slightly raised. I waited for my cue line, an awkward silence growing between us. A thought suddenly jolted in my head: *You have the first line, Jack!*

"WHAT A BEAUTIFUL CAPE!" I spit out quickly, not at all like I'd practiced.

I could tell I was rushing through the scene, apparently thrown by my false start, but when the intro to the song kicked in, I fell into my groove. I knew exactly how I wanted to perform it. I let my voice soar on the first chorus and nailed the bit where I sang "big tall terrible *lady* giant," tilting my head on the word *lady* in bewilderment. Halfway through the song something strange happened. I began to stop thinking about what to do next. As I sang these lyrics about adventure in a strange place, they began taking on a new meaning. I'd seen a lot of crazy things in the past few months, and while most were far less remarkable than beanstalks and castles, some felt no less terrifying. I began throwing away my planned acting beats, allowing my brain and heart to run free. I almost didn't want it to end. I took in a deep breath to prepare for the last note, the highest in the song, when my throat suddenly seized up.

"In the skyyyyyy-YYYY-yyy."

My voice cracked worse than anything I'd ever heard! I tried to stay in the moment through the remainder of the accompaniment, but I knew it was impossible to hide the embarrassed look on my face. I wanted to run offstage and down the high-school halls, through the parking lot and down the expressway past our house in Sussex Meadows. I wanted to keep running, all along the Ohio turnpike and up to 86th Street and into my old apartment in New York. I wanted to bury my face in my old bedroom pillow, praying that if I squeezed my eyes tight enough I'd wake up back in New York, realizing this whole Shaker Heights disaster was just a nightmare.

"Thanks for coming in, Jack," Renee said.

The next morning my brain felt like a melted ice-cream sundae. I sat in the living room crafting a barricade of textbooks, homework, my laptop, and breakfast around me, preparing for the fateful phone call.

"Are you sure you don't want to go up to your room? It's probably more comfortable," my mom asked, almost tripping over a bowl of oatmeal on her way to the kitchen.

"No, I like it down here," I said, glancing up from the same paragraph of *The Outsiders* I'd been rereading for half an hour. Suddenly, the phone rang, triggering a spike in my heart rate that could have been measured on the Richter scale.

"Hello," I said, trying to sound casual, my hand practically strangling the receiver.

"Hey, Jack!"

"Oh hey, Lou," I said, exhaling. "How's it going? You hear anything yet?"

Silence.

"I just did," she said slowly. "And . . . I got the part!"

"*Omigosh, omigosh!* That's awesome!" I cheered.

"Yeah, I'm so excited!" she said, giggling. "Please tell me we get to be scene partners!"

My excitement for Lou quickly turned to panic. What would it say about me if even the Shaker Heights Community Players thought I wasn't good enough?

"I can't say that yet," I said, pacing across the hardwood floor.

"Oh well, I'm sure your call is coming soon," she said quickly. "They're probably going alphabetically. Benning is before Goodrich."

"Yeah maybe."

"No, it is. B comes before G."

"No, I know. Yeah, maybe it's just alphabetical."
I was trying to convince myself.

"I'm sure that's it. They'd be crazy not to cast
you. You were so good!"

"I don't know," I said. "I'm guessing there was
at least one guy there who didn't crack on his high
note."

"It really wasn't as bad as you think."

That's what she'd said to me last night in the
lobby along with a lot of other really nice things.
I remained unconvinced.

"Lou," I said, dropping my voice. "I sounded like
a sheep getting electrocuted."

"C'mon," she said. "At worst it sounded like a
little tickle, but I'm sure you were still the best in
the bunch."

"Yeah, well, whatever," I said glumly. "It's okay
either way. I mean, I didn't even want to do it in the
first place, remember?"

I could feel Lou go cold on the other end.

"But hey," I added hastily. "I'm so excited
for you, and no matter what, you're going to be
amazing," I said, plopping myself back onto my pile
of pillows.

"Thanks, Jack," she replied. "Well, let me know if

you hear anything. Even if you don't get it, I'm glad you auditioned." She paused. "That took guts."

Just then call-waiting beeped in my ear.

I got it.

☆

"Jack's mom is going to pick you guys up at ten," Louisa's dad called through the window four days later. We hopped out onto the curb, scripts clasped firmly in our hands. "Text me if you get out early."

I gave a little wave and followed Lou up the stairs of the cathedral. It seemed a little strange to be going to a church this late in the day, but Lou explained that their rec room doubled as a great rehearsal space. Lou reached for the big wooden door but before letting me pass blocked the entrance with her body. "Still feeling like you *didn't want to do the show in the first place*?"

I laughed, pushing past her. "Yeah, that was just some garbage I made up to make myself feel better."

The rec room smelled of doughnuts and incense, not the typical smells of a first rehearsal but inviting nonetheless. The walls were lined with finger paintings, and in the center of the room, a circle of folding chairs, a few people already seated in them, chatting and highlighting their lines. I wondered how different this would be from a first rehearsal on Broadway. Was there going to be a model presentation of our set? Fittings with our costume designer?

"Hey, Lou." A young woman waved, approaching us. Lou's eyes lit up as she dove in for a hug. If I had to guess, I'd say the woman was in her early twenties, pretty in a rocker sort of way, with dyed-black hair and those spacers in her earlobes that always kind of freaked me out. "And you must be Jack," she said, turning her attention to me. I tried not to stare at her ears. "Wait, I just realized that's your name and, like . . . *your name.*"

"Ha-ha, yes," I said, extending my hand.

"Yeah, that's not gonna get old," she said, shaking it. "I'm Angela, your stage manager. Here's your first-day folder with the schedule and contact numbers and stuff. If you want to join the circle, Renee should be here soon."

Louisa broke off to hug some more people as I slowly found a seat in the circle. Not knowing anyone, I decided to read through my lines in the opening scene (as if I didn't already know them by heart).

"Wow, you know a lot of people." I smiled as Lou rejoined me, taking a seat.

"I know! I'm so excited. A lot of the *Music Man* cast is in this, too, including the Schwartzes," Lou whispered in my ear, tilting her head toward a cute elderly couple wearing oversize show sweatshirts—*Guys and Dolls* and *I Do! I Do!*, respectively. "They helped found the Players and have been in, like, every show since it started." She smirked. "Even if there aren't really any roles for them."

"Who are they playing in this?" I whispered. "Cinderella and Prince Charming?"

Lou snickered. "Oh look." She perked up in her seat. "The guy walking in is Wayne Flanagan," she said, nodding to a tall man in a vest who had big, wavy blond hair. As he entered the room, he slowly removed his sunglasses and looked up, doing a comedic double-take as if surprised to see people he knew.

"He's kind of dreamy." She sighed. "I've never done a show with him, but I've seen him as Bobby in *Crazy for You* and Sweeney in *Sweeney Todd*, so he can kind of do it all." She grinned. "He also owns that cute candle shop downtown."

"Cool." I smiled knowingly.

"And of course," Lou said, exhaling, "that's Denise Zook." She whispered it slowly, directing my attention to the woman entering the room. She was wearing a green blazer and knee-high leather boots, carrying the biggest iced coffee I'd ever seen. "She's like the star of Cleveland. She was our Marion in *Music Man*, Reno in *Anything Goes* and has won like four CLEVYs."

"*Clee-vies?*" I snorted.

"Yeah, like Tony Awards for Cleveland-area theater. If she's not playing the Witch, I'll be *shocked*. I'm kind of scared of her but so obsessed with her voice."

All of a sudden, everyone in the circle turned their attention to the doorway where a woman was handing a sleeping little boy to her husband. I recognized her as Renee Florkowski, the director from my audition. "What's her story?" I whispered to Lou.

"Well, she's a teacher in the musical-theater department at Baldwin Wallace. She actually directed in New York for a while but moved here to have kids or something. Now she only does one show a year, and it's always the best one."

As the cast gathered in their seats, Renee kissed her husband good-bye and strutted coolly to the circle. The room fell silent.

"*Opportunity is not a lengthy visitor,*" Renee declared. I recognized it immediately as one of Cinderella's lines. "Which is why I think we should dive right in." As she spoke, she began slowly circling the ring of chairs. "I'm Renee Florkowski, and I have the distinct privilege of welcoming you to the first rehearsal of *Into the Woods!*"

The cast broke into applause. I felt a rush of warmth in my chest. This was really happening. I was going to get to perform in my favorite show.

"I have to say, I was blown away by all of your auditions," she continued. "And I think we've assembled a group of actors who are going to be talked about for a long time. I'm happy to see a lot of familiar faces."

Out of the corner of my eye I saw Denise nodding deliberately. Wayne clasped a hand to his chest in fake shock as if saying, "*Who me?*"

"And some of you I just met last week," she said, stopping by Lou's and my chairs. "But your auditions inspired me, and I look forward to creating some first-rate theater together."

She looked directly into my eyes and gave me a little wink. I couldn't help but grin.

"Let's get started by going around the circle," she went on, walking into the center of the ring. "If you could say your name, what role you'll be playing, and how about . . . your favorite fairy tale."

As the cast introduced themselves, my excitement continued to build. Each person seemed friendlier than the next. Our Rapunzel's name was Sarah. She was a high-school senior who also lifeguarded at the city pool (there was a pool here!) and wondered if *True Blood* counted as a fairy tale. Cinderella was a cantor at the church we were rehearsing in and admitted to having recurring nightmares about *Rumpelstiltskin*. Dr. Krasnow, our Baker, was an optometrist and allergic to wheat. He joked about needing gluten-free pastry options as props, much to the horror of our stage manager, Angela.

I wasn't sure the last time I'd laughed this much. Probably months. It was fun being in a room of adults again. Even though I was twelve, I already felt more at home with these guys than I did with the kids in my class. It didn't matter that some of my cast worked as lawyers and real estate agents; we were all here for the same reason—we loved doing theater. My mind began to race, trying to remember everyone's names all the while planning what I'd say when it was my turn to speak. I was having such a great time that I'd almost forgotten about another cast, a thousand miles away, rehearsing for a different show. *The Big Apple* cast was probably already doing runs in costume, having woken up early that morning to perform on a talk show or concert in Bryant Park. I wondered what they'd think if they found out I was in a community theater production, but before I knew it, it was my turn to talk.

"I'm Jack," I said. "And I'll be playing . . . Jack." A wave of laughter rang from the circle. I guess Angela was right. "I know it's totally unoriginal, but my favorite fairy tale is *Jack and the Beanstalk*." I looked around the circle. Everyone was beaming, all seeming genuinely interested in what I had to say. Lou reached over and gave my arm a friendly little squeeze. "This is my first show with the Players," I continued, "and I'd just like to say I'm really happy to be here."

Chapter

Twelve

-LOUISA-

In an instant my life had gone from fine to *awesome*. Getting the phone call telling me I had won the part of Little Red was as good, if not better, than when my parents told me they would pay for a week at Camp Curtain Up. And then when Jack found out that he got cast, too . . . I don't think I stopped smiling until I fell asleep that night. I might have actually kept smiling in my sleep.

Once rehearsals for *Into the Woods* began, it was funny to think that the only thing I'd wanted to do a few weeks earlier was avoid Jack Goodrich at all costs, because now we were together all the time. Even so, I felt like there were two versions of

the same person: School Jack and Rehearsal Jack.
School Jack was like an alter ego: an unassuming
and neutral kid intent on averting the attention
of his classmates, while Rehearsal Jack was like
a superhero: a talented and extroverted actor
whose superpower was making friends instantly.
Meanwhile, I felt like his super sidekick, sworn
to protecting his secret. We both knew everyone
at school would eventually find out that he was
doing *Into the Woods*—half the town came out
to see the Players' productions, especially the
musicals. But Jack wanted to fly under the radar
as long as possible, and I wasn't about to break the
promise I'd made to help him do just that. Still, I
liked Rehearsal Jack much better than School Jack.
Rehearsal Jack was a lot of fun.

Every night, as soon as our kitchen clock read
6:45 p.m., I would scarf down the last bites of
dinner, grab my rehearsal bag, and run out of the
house to find Jack waiting by our car, having shed
his shy alter ego in favor of his outgoing superhero
identity. We'd spend the ten-minute ride to St.
Joseph's reviewing what we'd worked on the night
before, warming up our voices in the backseat. Dad
would tease us from the driver's seat, saying we

sounded like a flock of geese. When we got there, we'd sprint through the double doors and up the stairs to the rec room, where Jack and I would high-five and air-kiss our fellow cast members like we were guests at a cocktail party.

Wayne Flanagan, handsome as a movie star with his wavy blond hair, always stood by the water cooler filling up his Klean Kanteen bottle, so we'd say hello to him first. One of us would ask him to name the weirdest scented candles he'd sold at Wax & Wayne that day, and he'd respond by making up the worst smells imaginable. "Wet Dog," he'd joke. "Car Exhaust. Tennis Shoe."

From Wayne we'd move on to demand hugs from Mr. and Mrs. Schwartz, even when their matching show sweatshirts were covered in crumbs from the tray of brownies or crumb cake they'd be cutting up to serve during our mid-rehearsal break. Sarah, our Rapunzel, liked to pretend we were celebrities and asked us for our autographs, while Simon, Rapunzel's Prince, would pretend to restrain Sarah like she was a crazy fan. (It was totally obvious that Simon had a crush on Sarah.) It was usually around the time that Simon had his arm around Sarah's waist that Angela (who totally had a crush on Simon), would announce that we were starting, and Renee would lay out the evening's agenda.

I felt comfortable around everyone except for two people: Renee and Denise. As easy as it was for me to make jokes with Wayne Flanagan or hug Mrs. Schwartz, the thought of cracking a joke to Renee— or worse, making physical contact with Denise— made me shiver. It's not that either one of them was mean; they spoke to me just like they spoke to the adults. Maybe that's what freaked me out—they treated me like such a *grown-up* that I wasn't used to it. Plus they were both so smart. Renee knew exactly how to get what she wanted from you— like, she'd always pay you a compliment before giving you an acting note, or she'd suggest an idea in a way that made you feel like you came up with it yourself. And Denise was always asking super smart questions, wondering about her character's "intention," "sense of urgency," or "arc."

On the fourth night of rehearsal, as Denise was about to sing "Stay with Me"—a beautiful, sad song that the Witch sings to Rapunzel to keep her from leaving—I confided in Jack.

"They're both so intimidating, don't you think?"

I whispered, watching Denise and Renee discuss the scene as they used phrases like *remain active, raise the stakes,* and *fight self-indulgence.*

Jack looked at the two of them, then back at me.

"Why?" he asked. "Because they use fancy actor words?"

"Because they just seem so . . . *professional.*"

As soon as the word came out of my mouth, I realized why Jack didn't share my feelings of insecurity. He had just left a world full of professionals—he himself *had been* a professional—so people like Renee and Denise were completely familiar to him. I'm sure people in New York were even *more* intimidating.

Jack furrowed his brow like he was thinking hard about what I'd just said.

"They're taking the work seriously, sure," he conceded, "but there's no reason for you to be intimidated by them."

"I dunno," I said, "I don't think I've ever seen either of them *laugh.* They seem to take *everything* so seriously."

"C'mon, they have to laugh," Jack assured me. "They do musical theater. You can't do musical theater and not laugh."

"So says you," I muttered as Denise began to sing.

Jack gave me a quick glance and what I thought was a little smirk, then settled back in his chair to listen to the Witch's mournful appeal to Rapunzel.

A hush fell over the room as Denise's final note faded into silence, curling like a wisp of smoke around our ears. Chills ran up and down my spine; her performance of the song had been perfect, and I was more in awe of her than ever. I looked over to see tears in Renee's eyes. She opened her mouth to speak, but before any sound could come out, Jack's voice cut through the silence. Bold as a seagull swooping in on a dropped french fry at the beach, he said: "Wow, that was *so great*, Denise. I think as soon as you learn to sing on pitch and change all of your acting choices you'll *really* have something."

I could have fainted. Denise had probably never heard a comment like that in her lifetime. She stared blankly at Jack, her mouth opening and closing like a fish. The rest of the room followed suit in its speechlessness. *Had Jack lost his mind?* If I hadn't been so dumbstruck, I would have asked him. What seemed like an endless awkward moment was finally interrupted by Jack's big grin—one I had begun to know and adore. In the split second that everyone realized he was kidding, the energy of the room exploded. Tears welled up in Renee's eyes and now ran in steady streams down her cheeks as she howled with laughter, and Denise, continuing the joke, responded with, "Thank you so much, Jack. I really value your feedback." She then pretended to write a note in her music: "Learn. To. Sing. On. Pitch."

As Angela tried to regain control of the room—"Okay, everybody, we should probably get back to work . . ."—Jack turned to me, an expectant look on his face.

"I can't believe you just did that," I said, giggling.

"I know, that could've totally backfired," he said, his eyes flashing. "But it didn't, and now you know that Renee and Denise can laugh. So you don't need to be intimidated by them anymore."

My giggles subsided as Jack's words sunk in.

"Wait—you did that *for me*?"

"Well, yeah," he said, shifting in his seat. "You're my friend, so . . ."

So? No friend, not even the ones I made at camp, had ever found such a bold way to make me feel better about something.

If I thought Jack and I had been getting along before that night, it was nothing compared to the days and weeks that followed. Our newly solidified friendship became a full-time commitment.

Even when we weren't physically in the same room (which was rare), we were connected, texting or tweeting each other lyrics from the show:

"The carriage is waiting, we must be gone!"

"You can't just sit here dreaming pretty dreams!"

"Go to the *wood*!"

With our phones we'd take abstract photos of things from rehearsal that were nearly impossible to identify, then post them on Instagram—a secret guessing game of sorts. My favorite picture was a close-up of our prop cow's nostril that Jack took. I must have stared at it for at least twenty minutes before I figured out what it was.

And we'd leave voice-mail messages for each other in which we'd pretend to be Renee and give each other ridiculous notes, like when Jack left me this message:

"*Hi*, Louisa, it's *Renee*. Listen, great stuff today, but I want to give you a couple things to think about for tomorrow's rehearsal. This might sound crazy, but why don't you try wearing some *fake teeth*? And maybe use a Russian *accent*?"

To which I responded:

"*Hi*, Jack, it's *Renee*. Listen, you are doing some *terrific* work in the room, but may I suggest eating a lot of *beans* before our next rehearsal? It might connect you more to the *magic* beans in the story, and the gas you'll get will only give you more *layers* to work with."

At school, Jack skillfully maintained his low profile, and I continued to play along. That is, until the day Jenny got annoyed.

"Why didn't you text me back last night?" she demanded one Friday before history. We were nearing the end of our third week of rehearsals, and I had not spent any time with her.

"I was in rehearsal until really late, Jenny, I'm sorry—" I began.

"This is like the fourth time it's happened this week," she said, accusingly.

"I've been so busy—"

"Whatever, Lou—I texted you at, like, eighty thirty, and then I saw you were tweeting at nine during your rehearsal to someone whose handle is @GetRichJack, so I know you had your phone on you."

Oops.

"I'm really sorry—"

"Is @GetRichJack *Jack*?" Jenny asked, sliding into her desk behind me.

I took a deep breath, turned around in my seat, and leaned in close across her desk so only she could hear me.

"Yes," I whispered.

Her eyes widened.

"Why are you tweeting Jack about *Into the Woods*? I thought he gave up theater."

Jenny waited for a response, her lips pursed tight. She was clearly in no mood for apologies, and a lie would only make the situation worse, so I opted for the truth.

"He's in the show with me." I was speaking as quietly as I could. "He's playing the role of Jack."

Jenny scowled, piecing together recent events.

"Is that why he's not on the soccer team?" she asked, getting louder. "It wasn't because he 'hurt his knee'?"

"Shh," I said, looking around me, nervously. "His knee is fine. He just doesn't want anyone to know about the show yet."

Jenny squinted at me with suspicion. She did not like having secrets kept from her. Especially if they were mine.

"So, what's the deal?" she asked, after a moment. "Is he, like, your boyfriend now?"

"No!" I hissed. "We're just friends, I swear."

"Well, lucky him," Jenny said, her voice thick with sarcasm. "Does he know that the only reason you like him is because you're obsessed with all things Broadway?" She was getting louder as my heart beat faster.

"That's not true—"

"This is sort of perfect for you, right?" Jenny said, the anger rising in her voice. "If *you* can't be on Broadway, then you'll just kiss up to someone who has been."

"Who's been on Broadway?" Tanner Falzone's gruff voice knocked the wind out of me like a blow to the chest. I turned to face him, my thoughts racing, and I heard Jenny's barely audible, "Oh no..." An already unpleasant situation had just become much worse, as the very thing I had sworn to Jack I would protect was now dangling like a carrot in front of Tanner's eager face. I prepared to answer his question by making up a distant cousin named Heidi who I only saw every other Thanksgiving, but suddenly the sound of Jack's voice from the doorway, quiet but strong, surprised me once again:

"Me," said Jack. "I've been on Broadway."

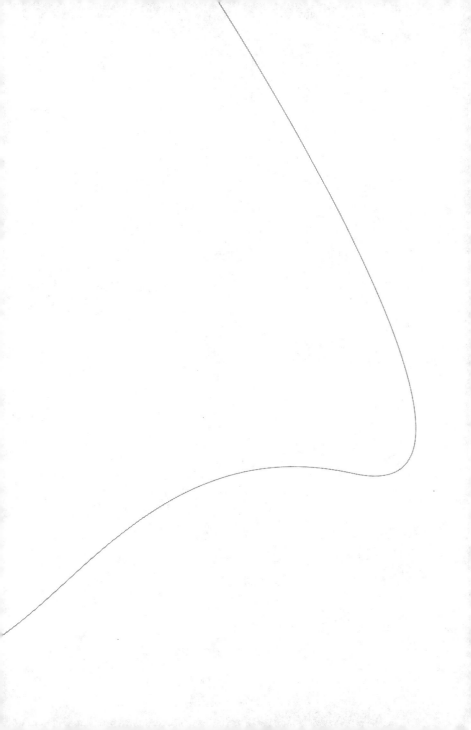

Chapter

—JACK—

What had I done? Everyone stared at me with the blankness of a thousand unfinished work sheets. Perhaps it was the confidence of a great week of rehearsal or perhaps it was not wanting to leave my friend (the only person who'd consistently been my cheerleader) hanging out to dry. Whatever caused my lips to utter these words didn't matter at this point. All that was certain was my cover had been blown, and I'd been the one to do it.

"I've been," I repeated. "I'm not a star or anything, but yes, I've been on Broadway."

The room was so silent, I could hear the scratch of chalk on a blackboard from the room next door.

I'd always heard confessing a secret felt like a weight being lifted off your shoulders. Right now it felt more like being bound into a life-size rubber-band ball. I braced for a spitball or apple core to blast me in the face, but what flew through the air was worse than anything that could have been thrown.

"That's so *gay*," Tanner grunted.

The word hung in the air like a bad smell. For such an obvious insult it still felt like a punch to the gut. I hated that word. Not for what it actually meant, but the power it seemed to give the person using it.

"Oh, grow up, Tanner," a voice muttered from the clump of classmates.

Everyone turned in shock, looking to see who was stupid enough to talk back to the biggest kid in seventh grade. I knew immediately whose voice it was. Tanner jerked his head back and forth in disbelief.

"What did you say?" he growled at Lou.

"Yeah, grow up," another voice chimed in. This voice I recognized as Jenny's. "What have *you* done in your life that's that impressive?" she challenged in a shaky, but piercing voice.

"Other than the third grade . . . twice!"

"Oohhhhhhhh!" a chorus of classmates blasted out in unison.

I wasn't sure whether to burst out laughing or run and hide in the bathroom. Tanner's mouth hung open, his face turning hot-sauce red. I figured I'd better step in before things got too messy.

"Hey, it's cool," I said, entering the room. "Yeah, guys, I used to do theater. Still do, actually." I nodded quickly to Jenny and Lou, a simultaneous *thank you* and *I'll take it from here*. "But, Tanner"—I cleared my throat—"I'm sure there are a lot of things you can do that are *really* impressive."

"Yeah, like destroy you and your little ballet friends," Tanner snarled back at me.

Oh boy, I thought. My eyes darted to the doorway. Where the heck was Mrs. Lamon?

"I'm sure you could. No question about that." I laughed nervously. This was a disaster. I'd gone from having my feelings hurt to fearing the actual possibility of broken bones. "Look, you've got your stuff. We've got ours. Isn't it cool that we can all . . . get along?" I said, realizing how corny and Sesame Street my words sounded.

"What did you do on Broadway?" a boy's voice

called out from the group surrounding Tanner. It was Sebastian, an athletic kid I recognized from soccer tryouts. He was tall and popular and probably Coach Wilson's first pick for the team. "Were you in *Book of Mormon*?"

Tanner turned to him in disgust as if asking *What are you saying? We need to put this kid to shame.*

"What?" Sebastian defended casually. "My dad took me to see that at Playhouse Square. It's by the *South Park* guys."

"No, I wasn't in *Book of Mormon*," I jumped in quickly, seizing the opportunity to change the subject. "But, that's cool your parents let you see it. Mine said I had to wait until I was in high school. On Broadway I was in . . ." *Oh man*, I thought. Why couldn't I have been in a show that sounded really manly like *Rocky* or *Jersey Boys* or at least something without the word *Mary* in it? "Um, *A Christmas Story* and *Mary . . . Poppins.*"

"Shut up! I love *Mary Poppins*!" a pretty blond girl named Jessica chimed in. It was the first time I'd ever heard her speaking voice. "Did you get to ride up the banister?"

"No. Well, not during the show." I shrugged. "But

one of the stagehands let me ride it on my last day. It was pretty sweet."

"*It was pretty sweet,*" Tanner repeated in a mocking high-pitched voice. This kid was ruthless.

"Make fun of him if you want," Lou said, squeezing her way up to his desk, hands planted on her hips, "but when he was on Broadway, Jack was making more money . . . *than your dad.*"

Tanner looked to me and tensed his face. *This is it*, I thought. I should just surrender to two long years of swirlies and locker coffins. I wondered if my parents would actually consider moving back to New York if I came home with a black eye. "Is she for real?" Tanner asked me after a long silence.

"Um," I murmured. "I'm not sure what your dad does. Probably something really fancy, but I guess I . . . did make a pretty big paycheck."

Tanner's eyes narrowed, sizing me up. "That is so"—he took in a deep breath, preparing his attack—"weird."

Weird I could do. To be honest, I couldn't agree more. As an actor you're asked to dance across the stage singing in kooky costumes often wearing dead people's hair. Not exactly a typical middle-school occurrence.

"So you got to spend all that money?" Sebastian asked, drifting away from the group of boys surrounding Tanner. Truthfully, I didn't. My parents used some of it to pay our rent. Some of it went to my agent, and the rest they put in a bank account that I couldn't touch until I went to college. At the end of the week I'd get an allowance of twenty dollars, which I'd usually spend on chips or candy or something sweet my parents never allowed in the house.

"Yep. I totally did."

Okay, I lied a *little*.

"I was even going to buy a pool for my rooftop," I continued. "But I decided they were too much work."

Okay, maybe more than a little.

Hey, whatever! So my life in New York more closely resembled an average preteen's than a rapper's in a music video, but it couldn't hurt to pretend. Lou looked at me inquisitively, as if asking *Really?*

Shh, I'll tell you later, my eyes broadcasted back. She nodded knowingly. I could tell we'd been spending a lot of time together. You knew you had a good scene partner when they could read your mind with a single look.

"Sorry, class." We heard Mrs. Lamon's voice as she came tearing in from the hallway. *Saved.* "The copy machine was broken and started spewing out hundreds of pages of . . . You know what? It doesn't matter. Can everyone take their seats and open your textbooks to page thirty-seven. The Boston Tea Party."

After school when the bus pulled up in front of my house, Lou and I hopped out together. My mother was wearing her *Christmas Story* ball cap, pushing our brand-new lawn mower across the overgrown grass. Originally my parents intended for lawn duty to be a part of my weekly chores, but a guardian angel (in the form of a sales associate at Home Depot) warned against anyone under age fifteen operating the mower. My mom waved to us, wiping her forehead with her new gardening gloves.

"I'm just gonna walk Lou to her door," I called out.

My mom nodded and started the mower up again.

"I'm sorry your secret got out," Lou apologized, kicking a pebble down the sidewalk. "Jenny was the only person I told, and even she didn't mean to let it slip. I was just being a bad friend to her, and then Tanner—"

"No, it's fine," I said, cutting her off. "I'm sure it would have gotten out eventually. It was stupid of me to try to keep it a secret in the first place."

We walked slowly down the tree-lined sidewalk, past the lawn with the rosebushes and that creepy garden gnome. "All things considered, it could have gone worse." Lou shrugged. "I mean, Jessica Wolfson acknowledged your existence. I've been in the same class as her since kindergarten, and I'm pretty sure she doesn't even know my last name."

"Yeah, it's cool. I just wonder what the fallout's gonna be with Tanner and his friends," I said. "I might as well start ironing bull's-eyes to the back of my shirts."

"I bet he's not going to mess with you," Lou responded. "He usually only picks on the kids with *lower* self-esteem than him. You obviously have a lot to be proud of."

I decided not to mention that being called gay

in front of my entire class made me feel pretty small.

"Besides," she continued, "he's too afraid one of your big-shot New York people will slap him with a lawsuit or something."

I chuckled, getting a mental image of Davina in a judge's robe with a powdered wig, banging that hammer thingy. *Aw-duh in the Cawt! Aw-duh in the Cawt!*

"Yeah, little does he know I still dig through couch cushions to find money to buy KitKats."

We turned up the walkway to her house. "Well, I'll see you soon," I said, stopping just short of her doorstep. "And seriously, thank you for standing up for me. That was really nice of you." I meant it.

She buried her fingers underneath the straps of her backpack.

"No one's ever put themselves out there for me like that," I said. "You're a pretty cool girl."

Lou smiled, and then to my surprise flung her arms around my shoulders, pulling me in for a hug. Her hair smelled nice, like apples. For a second all I could hear was the growl of our lawn mower humming in the distance. Suddenly, the sound cut out and was replaced by the bark of my mom's voice two houses down.

"Jack, hon!" she called out.

I pulled away from the hug.

"Yeah, mom?" I asked, turning away from Lou. My mom was walking toward the edge of our yard, pulling off her gardening gloves.

"Are you gonna be much longer? Because Davina left a voice mail that I think you're gonna to want to listen to."

Davina? What could Davina want? I wondered.

"Okay, Mom! Coming!" I turned quickly back to Lou. "Sorry, I should—"

"Don't worry about it." She grinned, shoving me playfully down the path. "Go listen to your voice mail. I'll see you at six forty-five." She skipped up the steps to her door and waltzed into her house without looking back.

I jogged down the pavement, sticking my tongue out at the garden gnome, leaped over a crack in the sidewalk, and ran up to our front door.

"What did Davina want?" I asked eagerly.

"The message is on the house phone," my mom said, wheeling the lawn mower up our driveway. "She's already out of the office and on her way back to Jersey, but we can call her first thing tomorrow." My mom looked back at me for a second. She had an expression on her face that I couldn't read. I knew when my agent called it was usually to deliver great news or something really bad. I dashed up the steps and pushed through the front door into the quiet of our house. I snatched up the house phone from the table by the stairs and froze, suddenly realizing I had no idea how to operate it. The idea of a landline was still new to me. No one in New York ever bothered with them. As I searched the receiver for an envelope icon, my mom popped her head in the doorway.

"Press pound and then dial your father's birthday."

Aha! I stamped out the digits and pressed speaker phone, catching my breath as the familiar husk of my agent's voice filled the room.

"Jack, honey. Listen."

Chapter

-LOUISA-

I had no clue who Davina was, but she must have been important enough for Jack's mom to walk down the street to tell him about her voice mail. Once I got to my room, I texted Jack: "Davina?! Can't wait to hear what *that's* about!"

Then I called Jenny. She answered on the first ring.

"I'm so sorry, Lou," she said meaningfully, "I should have chosen a more private place to be mad at you. I didn't think about how close Tanner's desk is to ours."

"It's okay," I replied, "Jack wasn't going to be able to keep his secret forever, and even though

Tanner was a jerk about it at first—"

"It kind of ended up being awesome," Jenny interrupted. "I mean, you were no joke, standing up to him the way you did."

"Yeah, you, too," I said. "We were kind of brave."

"'Kind of'? C'mon, we totally rocked! We just gave the biggest bully a royal smackdown in front of the whole class."

I couldn't help but smile at the memory of Tanner's confused and slack-jawed reaction when I told him about Jack's Broadway salary.

"I just wanted to say that I'm sorry, too," I said, remembering that offering Jenny an apology was the reason I'd called her. "I know we haven't hung out in a while. But I don't have rehearsal tomorrow, so—you wanna come over?"

Jenny never let herself get too excited about anything, which was how I knew she'd missed me because she squealed "Sure!" into the phone.

"Cool," I said. "I'll check with my parents, but I'm sure you can come over whenever you want."

We said good-bye, and I instantly felt an overwhelming sense of calm. While it was certainly comforting to know that Jenny was no longer mad at me, the thing I was most relieved about was that Jack didn't have to hide anymore. The two versions of Jack Goodrich could finally blend into one. We'd be able to talk about rehearsals at school now, and invite our classmates to see the show, and we wouldn't have to worry about how they'd react. Plus he'd called me a "cool girl," which, I have to admit, made me feel pretty great. I decided that some celebratory music was in order, and within minutes I was dancing like a fool, the cast album of *Kinky Boots* blasting from my speakers: *"Say yea-ea-ea-ea-eah! Ye-ea-ea-ea-eah!"* Yeah, indeed.

A few hours later, as I was finishing dinner, I checked my phone and realized that Jack had never texted me back. When I stepped onto our driveway at 6:45, he wasn't standing by our car. I dialed his number on my cell phone. After several rings, he picked up.

"Hey, slowpoke, we gotta go," I said, peering down the street to see if he was on his way.

"Uh yeah, sorry," Jack said, sounding distracted, "I was about to call you. My mom's gonna drive me tonight, actually."

Something in his voice made me nervous, but I

decided to ignore it for the moment.

"Oh okay," I replied. "How come?"

"She has a couple errands to run, so . . ."

He didn't finish his sentence. I waited a moment, then realized he was waiting for me to speak.

"Okay!" I said, forcing a friendly tone. "I'll see you there, then!"

In the car, Dad must have sensed something was wrong, because he asked, gently, "Did you and Jack have a fight?"

"No," I said, thinking *We had, like, the opposite of a fight.*

"Do you need me to pick you up after rehearsal?" he asked. "Or do you think Jack's mom will give you a ride as usual?"

I hadn't thought that far ahead.

"Y'know what?" Dad said. "Why don't you just text me later? Let me know what you need me to do."

"Okay," I said, as he pulled into St. Joseph's parking lot.

I was anxious to go inside, but also hopeful

that once Jack and I were in the same room again, chatting it up with our castmates, my concerns would be put to rest.

But Jack wasn't there when I arrived, so I had to make the social rounds by myself. I asked Wayne about his candles, and he responded with, "Where's your partner in crime?" Mr. and Mrs. Schwartz each gave me a hug, but not without asking, "Where's Tweedledum?" And Simon, instead of grabbing Sarah to keep her from asking for my autograph, simply said, "Wait—where's the other one?" As my cast's inquiries persisted, I grew increasingly uncomfortable. Jack's mom was just as punctual as my parents. Not only that, but Jack had told me that being late for rehearsal on Broadway could get you in a lot of trouble, and because of that he was always in the habit of arriving early. *So where the heck was he?*

Finally, as Angela called everyone to attention at 7:03 p.m. (I knew this because I kept checking my phone), Jack appeared in the doorway. I raised my hand to wave him over to where I was sitting, but he didn't even look in my direction. Instead, he remained in the doorway for a while, long enough to make it seem like he was deciding whether to even enter the room. Eventually he did enter, but with a weird hesitation, like a guy walking into an empty girls' restroom. I kept my eyes fixed on Jack as Renee detailed the order of scenes we'd be working on that evening, troubled by his vacant stare toward the floor. My stomach did a little jump when Renee said we'd be reviewing a scene between Little Red and Jack. Normally, I'd be excited for the two of us to work together, but given the dark cloud that seemed to be hovering over his head, I was less than eager. Nevertheless, I went straight over to Jack as soon as Renee was finished talking, hoping I could fix whatever was bothering him while Angela set up the room for the first scene.

"Hey, there," I chirped as I approached his chair.

Jack glanced up at me, then looked back down at the floor, which seemed to have a magnetic pull on his gaze.

"You want to run lines before we work on our scene?" I offered.

"No, I'm good with the lines," he mumbled, not looking up.

I took a deep breath and tried again.

"You missed the new candle scents," I said,

sitting in the chair next to his. "Wayne and I didn't want to play without you, but we still came up with a couple good ones. Leftover Chinese Food, Morning Breath . . ."

Jack abruptly got up from his chair. "I should get some water before we start."

My heart sank. Jack walking away from me mid-sentence was all the confirmation I needed that something was wrong. What made it worse, though, was my growing suspicion that I had something to do with it. But *what*? Had I said something to hurt his feelings? How was that possible, considering the day we'd just spent together? I racked my brain for clues. Only hours earlier we'd been a pair of heroes, standing up to the scariest kid in class. We'd felt triumphant and relieved on the bus ride home, he'd thanked me on my doorstep, and then we hugged . . .

Oh no. *The hug.* I had just meant it to be friendly, but maybe it had lasted a second too long; maybe I'd hugged him a little too tight. As I felt the blood rush to my face, another memory flash sent my head spinning: Mrs. Goodrich's voice, calling from the sidewalk, "*Davina left a voice mail that I think you're gonna want to listen to.*" It didn't occur to me when I texted Jack, "Davina?! Can't wait to hear what THAT's about!" that Davina might be his—gulp—*girlfriend*. A girlfriend in New York, whose voice-mail messages were obviously important. A fancy New York girlfriend who was probably on Broadway and would not want her boyfriend hugging a girl whose most impressive acting credit was a local commercial for A. J. Heil Florist. That would certainly explain why Jack would be freaked out, especially if he thought the intention behind my hug was—double gulp—*romantic*. (It wasn't romantic; it really was just a friendly hug. Like how I hugged Mr. and Mrs. Schwartz, but with less crumbs.) I watched for a moment as Jack filled up his water bottle across the room, then I turned away, mortified. I had to figure out a way to explain myself to him without making things even more awkward between us, but this was not the time or place. I would just have to wait out the next three hours.

The next three hours felt more like three years. Jack and I avoided each other the entire time, except for when we had to do our scene, in which

Jack shows Little Red the golden-egg-laying
hen. Little Red tells Jack that she doesn't believe
he could steal the golden harp from the giant's
kingdom, and she challenges him:

Little Red Riding Hood: Why don't you go up to
the kingdom right now and bring it back and show
me?

Jack: I could.

Little Red Riding Hood: You could not!

Jack: I could!

Little Red Riding Hood: You could not, Mr. Liar!

After our first pass at the scene, I knew it had
gone terribly, even before Renee pulled both of us
aside for a private discussion.

"Louisa," she said, consulting the notes on her
iPad, "I really like how committed you are to Little
Red's skepticism, but I felt like this time through
you were actually a little too aggressive toward
Jack. It's okay to challenge him, but you don't want
to scare him." *Too late*, I thought. There was so
much nervous adrenaline coursing through my
veins that I'd practically screamed all my lines.

"And, Jack," Renee continued, "you seemed

sort of passive. I think in this scene it's important to you that Little Red not only believe you, but respect you." Renee looked down at her iPad. "And you want her to like you." Jack just nodded silently, looking down at his beloved floor. I wanted to vomit.

When ten o'clock finally arrived, I realized with a sense of dread that I'd forgotten to text my dad about whether I'd need a ride home. As I collected my bag and script, trying to decide what to do, I heard Jack's tentative voice behind me.

"You need a ride, right?"

Mrs. Goodrich must have known something was up, because she was extra chatty as she drove us home, talking about the wallpaper she'd uncovered while repainting their bathroom, wondering aloud why the street lamps in our subdivision turned on so early ("Seems like a waste of energy"), asking me what garden-supply store my mom liked best. She filled the time impressively, making it easy for me and Jack not to speak to each other.

But as we turned onto our street, I felt a surge of courage. "You don't need to drop me off, Mrs.

Goodrich," I said, "I can just walk from your house."

"You sure?" Mrs. Goodrich asked, looking at me, then at Jack, in her rearview mirror.

"Yeah, it's fine," I said, rehearsing in my head what I was about to say to my friend. I could sense Jack tensing beside me. *Better to get this over with*, I thought, *otherwise it'll just get worse.*

Mrs. Goodrich pulled into their driveway and hastily went inside, leaving me and Jack alone. I suddenly realized that so many of our uncomfortable conversations had taken place on or near this driveway that we should put a sign out: "Awkward Spot." Jack turned to follow his mom.

"I don't want to be your girlfriend!" I blurted out. In my head it had sounded different, way less silly.

Jack turned back around, looking at me like I'd just announced I was from outer space.

"What?"

"I only hugged you because I was happy for you; I was happy that you didn't have to lie about who you were or what you were doing. I wasn't trying to get you in trouble with Davina, or steal you away from her, or anything like that. I mean, I like you, but I don't have a *crush* on you."

My words hung in the air like dust particles.
I wished for a strong wind to blow them, and me,
away.

After a painfully long pause, Jack finally spoke.

"Davina's my *agent*," he said softly.

"Oh." I felt relieved and humiliated all at
the same time. Davina *did* seem like a more
appropriate name for an agent.

"And I never thought you wanted to be my
girlfriend," Jack continued. "I didn't think the hug
was a big deal." I wondered why he wasn't laughing
by now, because the whole situation was feeling
pretty ridiculous. But instead of laughing, Jack just
looked miserable.

"So, then . . . what's *wrong*?"

Far off an ambulance siren whined,
interrupting the awful silence that followed my
question.

Chapter

–JACK–

"The producers of *The Big Apple* called to see if I could come in for a few weeks."

Lou froze, her feet halting their nervous shuffle.

"I'd be a vacation swing."

"A what?" Lou shot back quickly.

"It's a person who comes into the company but just for a little bit. I'd get to understudy Hudson, the role I was supposed to play."

She stared at me blankly, her lips quivering, failing to form words. I took her silence for confusion and decided to keep explaining.

"One of his understudies is out with mono, and the only other person who knows the role is about to go to his brother's wedding in San Diego. They want me to come in and be, like, the standby."

"So . . . you would be doing . . . what?" Lou's words slowly emerged from her mouth.

"Well, mostly watching the show or listening backstage on the monitor, you know, learning the part in case anything happened and I'd have to go on."

"So you wouldn't even be . . . *performing*?" Her voice flicked with an unexpected sting.

"Maybe I would." I shrugged, realizing this wasn't unfolding the way I'd hoped. "It would all depend. If something happened to Corey, the boy who took over for me, then I'd be the only one who could make sure the show would still happen."

She nodded slowly, then looked down at the driveway. "When would you have to leave?"

I felt a sinking in my stomach. No matter how I phrased my response, it was going to feel like a hundred Band-Aid rip-offs.

"Monday. And I need to let them know by noon on Sunday."

Lou was still for a moment, then shifted her gaze up to the night sky. I could tell her brain was going a mile a minute.

"I know what you're thinking," I mumbled. "I'd probably have to pull out of *Into the Woods*. You guys would be long into tech week, and it wouldn't be fair to make the cast act with an invisible Jack for three weeks."

"So, you've already made your mind up," she said, looking right at me and crossing her arms. "Am I right?"

"No, I haven't." My body suddenly felt like a roasting hot dog. I leaned up against the cool metal of the van door. "I have to talk to Davina at some point and discuss it with my parents."

Lou began fiddling anxiously with the zipper of her *Music Man* hoodie.

"I also wanted to talk about it with you," I continued. She let go of the zipper and buried her hands in the stretched-out pockets. "You're my only real friend here, and I realize it puts you in an awkward position. You're the reason I auditioned for *Into the Woods*. If it weren't for you, I'd still be kicking a soccer ball against the garage, feeling sorry for myself, and acting like a brat to everyone."

I looked for a nod of the head or a twinkle in her eye, something that would indicate a shred of understanding on her part. But Lou seemed more interested in the lint on her jeans than the friend standing in front of her.

"I thought you said you couldn't even do that role anymore," Lou muttered. I tried not to show on my face how much her words burned, knowing they were at least, in part, true.

"Yeah the singing's gonna be hard, but I think working on *Into the Woods* has helped with, like, my confidence and stuff," I said, shrugging. "I think without your help I'd never have been able to show my face in New York again."

The only sounds that could be heard were the chirping of insects and a hum coming from our garage lights. In my dream scenario this would be the moment where my theater buddy put her disappointment aside, hugged me, and remarked what a great opportunity this would be to heal the hurt caused by getting fired. Even in the second-most-desirable scenario, she'd beg me to stay, swearing that the show just wouldn't be the same with another Jack. But under the yellow glow of an October moon, in the shadow of a dusty minivan, my friend wouldn't even look me in the eyes. This was the girl who on my first day in Ohio interrogated every word that came out of my mouth. The girl who could talk for hours comparing Broadway musicals to their Hollywood adaptations. The girl who stopped at nothing to convince a boy she hardly knew to face his fears and audition for a musical. For the first time since we'd locked eyes that afternoon in August, Lou had nothing to say.

"Okay, well, we should get back to our houses before our parents send out a search party." I laughed phonily.

She nodded, turned away from me, and walked down my driveway toward her house.

That night as I lay in bed, one of Sondheim's lyrics tumbled in my head. It seemed to have floated from the pages of my binder and into my dozing thoughts. It was from the song "Giants in the Sky," in which Jack measures the fantasy world with the family he's left back home.

"And you think of all of the things you've seen, And you wish that you could live in between."

I flipped my pillow to the cool side, wishing for a way to return to *The Big Apple* without having to leave my *Into the Woods* family behind.

The next morning I sat at the breakfast table, drawing nervous spoon circles in my Greek yogurt. My mom dialed Davina's number.

"I think it will be good to talk to her directly," she said, passing me the phone. "Ask as many questions as you need."

I put the receiver up to my ear just in time to hear a familiar voice bellowing from the other end.

"Jack, honey, how are you, my sweets?"

"I'm good. How are you, Davina?"

"Excellent, Jack! I'm great! I'm at the vet right now. Chicken Poodle Soup's getting her teeth cleaned, and let me tell you, it's about time. I was starting to hide Tic Tacs in her Puppy Chow."

I laughed. This was classic Davina.

"So, listen, Marty and Fern from *The Big Apple* put in a call to me yesterday asking if you could come in for three weeks to vacation swing. Two thousand a week was their first offer, but I know what a bind they're in, so I squeezed out an extra two hundred fifty a week plus a moving bonus.

You'd rehearse for two days and start trailing Wednesday night."

"Um. All right," I muttered.

"Dylan's one of my clients, you know, out with mono for at least a month, poor little guy! His Broadway debut, too, and he'll have to enjoy it from his bedroom. But listen, this is great for you. I knew it wasn't the end of your journey with *The Big Apple*, and now you get to be there for opening night. I hear they're having the party at Madame Tussauds, that wax museum on Forty-Second? *Very chichi.*"

I clasped the phone with both hands. I hadn't realized I'd get to be there during opening. That would mean getting dressed up in fancy clothes and having my picture taken for a crowd of photographers. It also meant unlimited desserts and dancing with my castmates.

"That's great," I said.

"It's more than great, Jack. It's a second chance. Everyone loves a comeback, and this time, *you* get to be the guy who saves the day. Also: I'm working on getting a fridge for your dressing room."

I looked over to my mom, who was smiling. Out of the corner of my eye I saw the stack of *Into the*

Woods flyers Angela had given us the night before to distribute throughout the neighborhood. My heart instantly sank.

"Davina, there's one problem, though."

"A car service? I tried, Jack. You know I asked for it, but they said they won't budge on that one. Not even Vivian Cromwell is getting that."

"No, it's not that. I actually"—I swallowed hard—"I got cast in a show here! In Shaker Heights. I'm playing Jack in *Into the Woods* right now, and I just feel bad about leaving my cast on such short notice."

"Oh," she peeped. I'd obviously caught her a little off guard.

"Yeah," I continued. "We're about to go into tech week, and I'd have to drop out if we moved back to New York, which would probably make some people a little upset."

"Yes, I understand," she responded quickly. "That's very professionally minded of you, Jack. It's something I've always admired." She took a long slurp of something. "But Jack, listen, in this business second chances only come once in a blue moon, and do you know what?"

I waited for her to continue. The sound of her

breathing alerted me that she might actually be waiting for a response.

"What?!" I blurted out.

"I happened to have heard from a little birdie"—she suddenly slowed down her speech, pitching her voice into a higher, quiet whisper—"that a certain Tony-winning director has been planning a certain revival of *Into the Woods* for quite some time."

I felt my pulse quicken.

"So next year when they're casting the workshop, guess who will be on the phone day in and day out, making sure that Jack Goodrich is the first person they think of during auditions?"

"Um, yo-ou?" I sort of squeaked.

"You bet, and once that voice of yours finishes changing, I don't think there's a single boy in New York who'd make a better Jack."

I was speechless. I'd never considered the idea of playing Jack on Broadway.

"Speaking of which," she resumed her hurried pace. "Fern and Marty have talked to the music department, and they're okay with re-orchestrating your songs and dropping the key in case you had to go on as Hudson. That way you don't have to worry about beltin' out those high notes that were giving you a little trouble during rehearsals." She exhaled. "It really is the perfect scenario."

I felt sweat collecting on the receiver. My thoughts were swirling like water in a bathtub drain.

"So why don't you talk it over with your parents? See if this is something you want to do, and if you need, I'm more than happy to call the director of your Cleveland show and see if there's a way to break the contract."

"Oh, I don't think there's any contract," I said. "We're rehearsing in a church."

"Oh!" she squawked. "Well, then. Talk it over with your parents and have them call me back this afternoon. Okay, I have to go, my sweets. Chicken Poodle Soup just got out, and *oh heavens*, if they didn't put the cutest little bow in her hair."

"Okay, thanks, Davina," I said. "Good-bye."

"Good-bye, my love," she said, and hung up the phone.

My dad was now standing behind my mom with his hands on her shoulders. They looked at me expectantly.

"So, what do ya think, Jack Sprat?"

"Um," I said, collecting my thoughts.

"Just so you know," my mom cut in. "Whatever you decide, we're completely behind you. I don't start teaching at the university until January, so I could come with you to New York if you wanted."

"But if you decide you want to stay here and do *Into the Woods*," my dad chimed in, "we think that's great, too."

While it was awesome having parents who supported me no matter what, it might have been nice to have someone to blame this decision on. I knew either way I'd be letting down a big group of people. As I looked down at my yogurt, Davina's words echoed in my head.

Second chances only come once in a blue moon.

Chapter

-LOUISA-

I hardly slept Friday night, except for maybe a few hours during which I had a dream—a nightmare, really—about Jack.

We were onstage in the middle of a performance of *Into the Woods*—the scene in Act 2 where the Baker, Cinderella, Jack, and Little Red all figure out how they are going to kill the giant, and at the moment that Jack is supposed to say "And I will climb a tree and strike her from behind," a cell phone started ringing from his pocket. Even though we were onstage—in costume and in front of paying customers—he still answered it: "Hello?"

We all watched his face light up with

excitement as he exclaimed, "Are you kidding? I'm on my way!"

He hung up the phone, turned to the audience, and shouted, "I'm going back to Broadway, suckers! *All of your houses look the same!*"

Then he ran into the wings and disappeared.

Those of us left onstage just stared at each other, dumbfounded, until Miles Krasnow, who played the Baker, put his hand on my shoulder and said, "Seriously, Little Red—did you really think Jack would *stay*?"

I woke up and felt like screaming.

When I rolled out of bed on Saturday morning, exhausted from having tossed and turned all night, I was in as bad a mood as I'd ever been, so foul that my parents seemed downright scared of me when I entered the kitchen. They had tried to talk to me the night before when I came in, but I'd just told them I wanted to be alone and shut myself in my room for the night. Now, as I poured myself some cereal, I could not escape their concern. Mom cleared her throat and said, gently, "Lou, hon, do you want to tell us what's going on?"

"No."

"Maybe we can help?"

I started to feel a roar growing inside me.

"No."

"You'll probably feel better if you talk about—"

"Jack is going back to New York!" I exploded, slamming the cereal box down so hard that a few Crispix flew out onto the counter.

"He's going back so that he can wait for something to maybe *happen!"*

My parents stared at me, uncertain. They looked like a pair of campers trying to figure out how to deal with the bear outside their tent. Mom made another cautious attempt.

"Sweetheart, what does that mean—"

"He's leaving our *show to go sit backstage at a* Broadway *show! Not* be *in a Broadway show! Sit* backstage *at a Broadway show!"*

"Like an understudy?" asked Dad.

"Not even! He's gonna be a vacation swing!*"*

My poor parents. They had no idea what I was talking about. And the truth was, I didn't even know what I was talking about—not really. I had only half listened to Jack's explanation of what he was being asked to do—once he'd said he might be leaving, I'd kind of gone into shock. (Though I was pretty sure I'd still managed to hurt his feelings.

Again. I had gotten so good at that.)

"Lou, honey," Mom said, "we don't know what a *vacation swing* is—"

"Then look it up!" I screamed, storming out of the room. As angry as I was, I was surprised that neither one of my parents ordered me to come back into the kitchen to apologize. Normally, they would never let me behave that way. The fact that they just let me go almost made me feel worse.

Back in my room, I took my own advice and looked up "Vacation Swing" on my laptop. Ignoring links to discounted porch swings and "Swing Classic—Your Dance Vacation Destination!", I found a New York actor's blog describing his experience as a vacation swing for *Phantom of the Opera*. He explained that it was a lot like being an understudy—you had to learn an entire part (sometimes more than one), and be ready at a moment's notice to perform. But what made it different was that it was only a temporary job, just as Jack had said. Vacation swings had to learn everything that the full-time understudies did, but they were only needed at the theater for a short amount of time—sometimes for only a week. Vacation swings were like an extra insurance policy for the show. I decided it didn't make sense why Jack would want to work so hard for so little payoff.

My phone rang, and Jenny's name popped up on the screen. Shoot. I'd forgotten about our plans. I must have done a poor job of concealing my grumpiness because as soon as I said, "Hey," Jenny launched into crisis mode.

"Oh my God—what happened?" she asked, adopting her most serious tone.

Jenny prided herself on being a good problem solver. She came up with a great plan B when it rained on my tenth birthday, suggesting that we clear out the furniture from our finished basement and host an "indoor picnic" instead of a barbecue in our backyard.

I hoped that she'd offer some kind of solution now. But when I finished explaining to Jenny what had happened with Jack, she was silent.

"Wow, that sucks," she said, finally.

"I know—so what should I *do*?" I waited for her to outline a plan.

Instead all she said was, "I don't think there's anything you *can* do. Except forget about it."

"What if I can't?"

"You have to!" Jenny commanded. "But let me help. My mom just bought me and my sister a manicure set. And since my sister bites her nails constantly, it's really *my* manicure set, so I'll bring it over. You should try 'Bond with Whomever.'"

"*What?*"

"That's the name of a nail polish color," Jenny clarified. "It's lavendery."

I looked down at my nails. There wasn't a nail polish color on the planet that could make me feel better, but I appreciated Jenny's offer to Bond-Me-with-Whomever. It seemed fitting, considering I'd bonded with Jack, a traitor. "Whomever" couldn't disappoint me more than he had.

"Okay," I said, miserably, "see you soon."

I knew I had to apologize to Mom and Dad before Jenny came over, so I went back downstairs and found them still in the kitchen, drinking their coffee.

"Sorry," I said, sheepishly. I realized I hadn't eaten my cereal. The bowl remained on the counter, quietly reminding me of the embarrassing tantrum I'd thrown.

Mom got up from her stool, wrapped her arm around my shoulders, and buried her nose in my hair.

"You ready to talk?"

Twenty minutes later, I felt like I was in an episode of *Dr. Phil*. Mom, Dad, and Jenny were all sitting on the couch in our living room, while I sat in an armchair facing them. Between us on the coffee table was Jenny's manicure set, its contents spilled out across the glass top. Jenny had wasted no time and was already pushing back her cuticles with a rounded metal tool.

"Do you know for sure that Jack is leaving?" Dad asked.

"He said he hasn't decided, but I'm sure he's going to choose New York," I said, curling my feet up underneath me. Mom jumped in.

"I think, for the sake of moving forward, we should assume Jack is leaving," she said, using her most reasonable voice. "Louisa will not be upset if he stays, obviously. She will be upset if he leaves, however, and so helping her manage that pain is how we can be most useful."

Dad tried to suppress a grin and failed. Mom turned to face him.

"What are you smiling at, Doug?"

"I'm just glad to see that you're putting your psychology studies to good use," he said, squeezing Mom's knee. "People will come far and wide for therapy sessions with you."

"Doug, do not make fun of me—"

"I'm not! I'm serious, Hannah—you're impressive!"

As they giggled, Jenny shifted uncomfortably and shot me an impatient look. She held up a nail file and waved it around as if to say, *Can you please wrap this up?*

"Hey, guys?" I interrupted. "Can we get back to *me*?"

Mom turned back to face me. She was blushing.

"Sorry, sweetie. Of course we can."

The session resumed.

"Are you having trouble understanding *why* Jack would go back to New York?"

I wanted to say yes, but the truth was—I totally understood why Jack would go back. Sure, he'd be standing by for someone playing the role he was originally *supposed* to play, but it was on *Broadway*.

How could I blame someone for choosing what I'd only been dreaming about my entire life?

"No, I get it."

"Okay, then," Mom continued. "Are you maybe a little jealous of him?"

Ugh, of course I was jealous. It was such an ugly feeling, but I couldn't deny that it was there.

"A little, yeah."

"It's perfectly natural to feel that," Dad chimed in, "but you can't let that cloud how you feel about him as a friend, you know? Jack's not about to make a decision to intentionally hurt you or make you jealous."

"I know."

"So why don't you tell us what upsets you the *most* about Jack leaving?" Mom asked, getting to the heart of the matter.

I didn't answer right away. I could have said that I was upset because Jack made a commitment to the Players. That someone else would have to be cast in his role, and that he (or worse, *she*) would have to learn the part in a really short amount of time. I could have said that I was upset that Jack's time in New York would most likely be wasted backstage, where he'd sit in a little room and *listen* to a Broadway show through an intercom. And sure, I could have said jealousy—that I'd never had to choose between two shows before, let alone a *Broadway* show, and the fact that he did get to choose just reminded me of how different we were, even though the last few weeks made it seem like we were pretty similar. I could have said any of those things, but none of them was the truth. What upset me the *most* about Jack leaving came out in a whisper.

"I just don't want to do *Into the Woods* without him."

And as soon as I said it I started to cry.

Jenny dropped her nail file, leaped from the couch, and threw her arms around me. Rather than tease me about having a crush on Jack, she just said, "Of course you don't!"

Mom got up and returned with tissues.

Dad waited for my sniffling to subside, then offered one perfect piece of advice. "Then I suggest you tell him how you feel," he said, "and still be prepared to let him go."

At eleven o'clock on Sunday morning, I knocked

on the Goodriches' screen door. Jack appeared moments later. Upon seeing me, he hesitated.

"I'm not going to yell at you or anything," I said.

"Okay."

Jack opened the door and stepped outside. He looked tired, too.

"Have you called Davina yet?" I asked.

"Not yet. I've still got an hour."

I saw in his eyes how much he was struggling with the decision, so I wasted no time in letting him off the hook.

"If you go to New York, I'll understand," I said firmly. "I mean, I'll miss you. But if I were in your shoes, I would go."

"You would?" Jack seemed surprised.

"Probably," I said, feeling stronger in my conviction. "I mean, a new Broadway musical? C'mon."

Jack smiled shyly.

"Yeah, it's hard to say no to something like that."

"I know. So say yes," I replied. "The Players aren't going anywhere—you can do next year's musical."

Jack flashed me a mischievous look.

"What if they do *Chess*?"

I smiled.

"Well, then you'll have to wait two years. Unless you have a serious growth spurt in the next twelve months."

"Highly doubtful," Jack said, "but you never know." He paused, then asked in a more serious tone, "Won't they be mad at me?"

"Are you kidding?" I said. "Everyone will be so excited for you when they find out. The Schwartzes will probably suffocate you with hugs."

"Yeah," said Jack, chuckling, "I'll have to be careful."

"Oh!" I exclaimed. "And just think what Sarah and Simon will do!"

We started to crack up, picturing Simon wrestling Sarah to the ground as she screamed Jack's name.

"Do you think Denise will miss me?" Jack asked wryly.

"Nah, as soon as you're gone, she'll forget you were ever there!"

We collapsed on Jack's front stoop, howling.

As I fought for breath through my laughter, I realized that I'd been completely wrong. What I'd been most upset about was not the threat that Jack and I wouldn't get to do *Into the Woods* together—it was that we wouldn't be *friends* anymore. And with that realization came another: There was no longer anything to be upset about. I knew in that moment that no matter what Jack Goodrich decided, our friendship was solid.

Chapter

–JACK–

"Ladies and gentlemen, this is your five-minute call. Five minutes until the top of the show," a woman's voice called over the loudspeaker.

A chorus of playful shrieks trumpeted from the dressing room next door. If I had to guess, some of my castmates had spent more time delivering gifts and reading cards than doing their makeup and getting into costume. Rightfully so—it was opening night! My dressing-room station resembled something closer to a hotel gift shop than the backstage of a theater. Presents and flowers from my family and castmates decorated every square inch of my desk. Nana had sent me a beautiful bouquet of orange tulips. Unfortunately, I was unable to locate a vase, so they were currently chilling in an old Slurpee cup. My parents delivered a miniature bonsai tree with a giant silver balloon attached to it that read, "You're 50!" Mom and Dad had a running joke that because no one manufactured Opening Night cards, they'd instead try to find the most random gifts possible. (My favorite remains the "Congrats on the Adoption!" bear I got for my *Mary Poppins* opening.) Even Davina sent along her token Edible Arrangement that sat nesting in a pile of unopened envelopes. I was tempted to scarf down a juicy strawberry, but I'd be disobeying the first rule of backstage etiquette: No eating in costume. The strawberry would have to wait until intermission.

I looked in the mirror, growing giddy with excitement, marveling at the awesome costume they'd built for me in such a short time. This opening night was going to be like none other. When I did *A Christmas Story*, it was in its second season, so while our opening night was spirited, we already knew audiences were going to love it. By the time I joined *Mary Poppins*, it had been running for almost six years, so while *my* performance was an evening of firsts, for the other thirty cast members it was probably just another day at work. Yes, tonight was going to be special. This was a show I'd watched sprout from words on a page into a fully blooming production. And while the last six months had been a roller-coaster ride for me, tonight I was getting to prove to the world that I was here to stay.

I parted my hair down the center, clipped my microphone in with the precision of a surgeon, and tugged on my hat.

"Ladies and gentlemen, this is your places call. Places, please, for the top of Act One. Places, please, and have a great opening night!"

The backstage erupted into cheers. I took a swig from my water bottle, spit my half-sucked Ricola in the garbage, and pushed open the dressing-room door.

"Break legs, Jack!" my dresser, Margie, said, lugging a clothes basket of heavy dresses.

"You're gonna be amazing!" another cast member said, passing me, pushing bobby pins into the front of her wig.

"You too!"

I rounded the corner and began up the stairs.

"Knock 'em dead, Jack," our stage-right crew guy called, slapping my back.

"Thanks, Billy!" I replied.

The show curtain was still down, so our stage was scattered with cast members stretching and giving each other congratulatory squeezes and thumbs-up signs. I walked onto the stage, collecting my thoughts and silently mouthing my first lines of dialogue. I looked around; there was still one person I hadn't seen. Then from behind, I felt a hand rest on my shoulder. I spun around and was greeted by the friendliest face in the world.

Lou looked incredible: her embroidered cape was tied tight around her neck, her cheeks rosy with blush, and peeking out from her hood, a mane of perfect brown ringlets.

"I wasn't sure if I was going to see you before we started." I smiled. "I know you like to get in your zone."

"Yeah, I think I'm good now." She winked.

"Are you nervous?" I asked.

"A little bit. It's packed out there! I know it's bad luck to peek into the audience, but I was filling up my water bottle and totally couldn't help myself!"

"Well, I'm glad. Our show's gonna be amazing." I

grinned. "You're gonna be amazing."

"Thanks, Jack. You are, too."

I leaned in and gave her a hug, slightly crushing her basket in the process.

"Whoops." I shrugged. "I hope your pastries are all right in there."

"Oh, trust me, they are. They're those gluten-free ones Mrs. Schwartz brought in. They could withstand the apocalypse."

We burst out laughing. Denise, who had been meditating upstage, cleared her throat. A raised eyebrow was all it took to shut us up.

"Hey," Lou whispered, taking on a more serious tone. "I just wanted to say before we go out there, I'm really happy you decided to stay."

"I'm happy I decided to stay, as well." I smiled back.

I began thinking of all the things that had happened since our minivan pulled up to my Shaker Heights home—the not-so-subtle hint-dropping about auditions, the confrontation with Tanner, the laughing on my porch in the middle of a tough decision.

"Seriously," I said, "thank you, Lou, for, well . . . everything."

"Awww, it was nothing," she said playfully.

Our cast party that night wouldn't be as swanky as *The Big Apple*'s, but the people I'd get to hang with were the best colleagues any actor could ask for. I might not have gotten to do a fancy press line, but Sarah and Simon (now officially dating) would be on hand snapping pictures, giving us the full paparazzi experience. At the end of the day, a show was still a show, whether I played to an audience of thousands or to a handful of family and friends. It was the people I got to share it with that would make it unforgettable.

"Okay, we should get into our positions," Lou said as the backstage lights began to dim. "Break legs, friend." She smiled.

"You too, friend," I said back.

As I watched her exit the stage, I felt a surge of adrenaline rush through my body. It wasn't nerves like I'd felt before an audition. It was more like the tingle I'd get standing at the top of a diving board, toes curled over the edge, knowing the only way down was by taking a giant leap.

"House to half. House to full," Angela said from her station just off stage right. The rumblings of our audience settled into a silent whisper of anticipation.

"Cast, stand by," she said into her headset, a smile beaming across her face.

I took one last deep breath and got into place, kneeling by my papier-mâché cow.

As the curtain rose, our orchestra sprang to life. A spotlight came up on our narrator, Mr. Schwartz, as he said with conviction the four most magical words in the English language:

"Once upon a time . . . "

Woods

Once upon a time, composer/lyricist Stephen Sondheim and book writer James Lapine sat down to write a musical based on the fairy tales of the Brothers Grimm. That musical was *Into the Woods*, a magical retelling of Grimm's stories that shows what really happens after "happily ever after." *Into the Woods* first premiered at the Old Globe Theater in San Diego in 1986 and quickly moved to Broadway the following year. It opened at the Martin Beck Theater (now the Al Hirschfeld Theater) on November 5, 1987, and closed on September 3, 1989, after 765 performances. James Lapine also directed the musical, which was nominated for ten Tony Awards, eventually nabbing three: Best Score (Stephen Sondheim), Best Book (James Lapine), and Best Actress in a Musical (Joanna Gleason). The original Broadway cast featured several stage legends, including Bernadette Peters as The Witch, Joanna Gleason as The Baker's Wife, Chip Zien as The Baker, Kim Crosby as Cinderella, Ben Wright as Jack, and Danielle Ferland as Little Red Riding Hood. Since its original production, *Into the Woods* has been revived three times: once on Broadway in 2002 and Off-Broadway in 2012 and 2014. The film adaptation opened in cinemas in December 2014.

ACKNOWLEDGMENTS

This book would not be possible without Jordan
Hamessley's desire and willingness to take a
chance on two new authors. Thank you, Francesco
Sedita and Sarah Fabiny, for continuing with us
on this journey, and to Kate Navin and Joe Veltre
for seeing us through the process. Thank you to
our *Submissions Only* family for giving us the best
creative springboard we could ever imagine. A
lifetime of thanks to Chris Wetherhead (Kate's
mom) for her red calligraphy pen and unfailing
encouragement, and to Arnold Wetherhead (Kate's
dad) for the photographic reminders of a theatrical
childhood, and to Jeff Croiter (Kate's husband)
for always listening. Thank you, Lyric Theater in
Burlington, Vermont, for providing inspiration for
the Shaker Heights Players. Thanks to Rory Bolger
and the late Susan Keenan (Andrew's parents)
for uprooting their life in Detroit, Michigan, to
pursue the acting dreams of their children in
New York City. Thanks to Ben Fankhauser for his
Shaker Heights expertise, and to Neal Hunter
Hyde for always being so helpful. Thank you,
Second Stage, for providing your beautiful theater.
Finally, thanks to all the directors, teachers, and
arts educators who continue to inspire future
generations of performers and theater-goers.

And now, a peek behind the curtains at

Jack & Louisa

ACT 2

Chapter

One

Everything was smaller than I had expected. More compact. The hallways were narrow, the ceilings low, the rooms tiny and warm from the mirror lights. But the sweet, musty smell was the same as any theater's backstage, and I couldn't decide what was more exciting—the things that surprised me or the things that were so familiar.

If I'd been told four and a half months ago that I'd be getting a guided tour of a Broadway theater from a former Broadway star who also happened to be my new best friend, I never would have believed it. And now here I stood, as close to my dreams as I'd ever been, *still* not quite believing it.

"You okay, Lou?"

I turned to see Jack looking at me, amused. He must have known I was overwhelmed.

"Yeah," I replied, thinking how interesting my life had become since Jack Goodrich moved in down the street from me.

In November, Jack and I had finished our run of *Into the Woods* with the Shaker Heights Community Players. The critic for the *Sun Press* had given it a glowing review: "Utterly enchanting," he'd gushed. "Poignant . . . Beautifully acted and sung by a stellar cast."

"I guess you're used to getting reviewed by, like, the *New York Times*," I'd said to Jack after reading the review to him over the phone.

"Are you kidding?" Jack had replied, incredulous. "A rave is a rave. Who cares who's writing it?" I loved that he felt as proud of our show as I did.

Speaking of proud—not only did our entire seventh-grade homeroom come to see our show, but they all stood during the curtain call when Jack and I took our bows! Even Tanner Falzone, who had made Jack a target of his ridicule early in the school year, whistled through his teeth like he was at a football game.

For the week following our run, it seemed like all of Shaker Heights was talking about our production of *Into the Woods*. I felt like a mini celebrity, like when the manager at Yours Truly Restaurant recognized me.

"Oh my god, you were so good as Little Red Riding Hood!" she exclaimed as she helped the hostess seat me and my parents. "So feisty." When our entrees were cleared about an hour later, a complimentary brownie sundae was sent over.

"Woo-hoo, star treatment," my dad said, grabbing one of the three forks provided and digging into the whipped cream. "I could get used to having a famous kid."

At the dentist, the dry cleaner's, the drugstore, people would come up to me to tell me how much they loved the show.

The same thing was happening to Jack, and I asked him if that's what it was like for working actors in New York.

"Not really," he said. "There's, like, eight million people there, and most of them don't go to

Broadway shows—tourists do. So it's pretty easy to be anonymous." We laughed at how much more famous he felt in Shaker Heights, Ohio, than he ever had in New York City.

Soon enough, though, our celebrity status faded away, brownie sundaes came with a price tag, and we went back to being regular seventh-graders. Our next shot at the spotlight wouldn't be until second semester, when Mrs. Wagner, our music teacher, would be directing a production of *Guys and Dolls*. I was looking forward to it, of course, especially since the part of Adelaide was on my list of dream roles, but as far as Mrs. Wagner was concerned . . . Well, let's just say that she wasn't the greatest director. Her only objective was making sure that everyone could be seen and heard on stage at all times, which usually meant scene after scene of kids standing in a straight line, delivering their dialogue very loudly to the audience instead of to each other. She was certainly no Renee Florkowski, our *Into the Woods* director.

So sure, we had a show on the horizon, but it wasn't going to be anything like what we'd just experienced with the Shaker Heights Community Players. And it didn't really matter, anyway. By early December, everyone had other things demanding their attention, like getting ready for the holidays.

"My parents and I are going to New York for New Year's," Jack announced one night while we were at his house doing our English homework. We were supposed to be answering questions about S. E. Hinton's *The Outsiders*, a book title that was suddenly hitting a little too close to home.

"Wow," I said, trying to conceal that jealousy, "how long are you going for?"

"Five days. We're staying with my parents' friends on the Upper West Side," Jack replied casually. After all this time, it still bugged me how easy it was for him to talk about New York— like he was talking about a corner store or a gas station.

"Are you going to see any shows?" I asked, staring at a page from my book but not reading a word.

"Probably," Jack said. "I have some friends

working right now who I should go support."

Friends to support! On Broadway! I mean, I always went with Jenny's parents to her yearly ballet recital in Cleveland, but—no offense to Jenny—that just didn't sound as cool.

"What are *you* doing for the break?" Jack asked, looking up from his homework. I hesitated, mortified to tell him.

"Um, not much. My uncle Dan and his girlfriend, Tina, are driving up from Missouri to visit for a couple days. She, um . . . really wants to see the Rock and Roll Hall of Fame." Jack wasn't a good enough actor to mask his pity. And I wasn't a good enough actor to mask my gloom.

I spent the next couple of weeks trying not to think about how different our winter vacations were going to be, choosing instead to concentrate on schoolwork and reminding myself that Uncle Dan made really good French toast. I'd never met Tina, but Dan had told me on the phone that she'd really liked the movie *Chicago*, so we'd "have lots to talk about" when they got to town. I wasn't convinced.

For the most part, Jack did a good job of not talking too much about his upcoming trip, probably sensing that it was a painful subject for me.

That is, until one day when we were riding the bus home from school and his cell phone chimed with a new text message. As he read the message, he let out a slight gasp and said, "I can't believe it—my mom just got me a ticket to see *Let's Make a Toast!*"

My heart sank. Jack and I had been obsessing over that show since we'd found bootleg clips of it on YouTube. It had recently opened on Broadway and starred the amazing Madeleine Zimmer, who Jack knew *personally*. I didn't want to ruin Jack's excitement, so I mustered a "That's amazing!" and tried not to burst into tears.

As the bus pulled up to our stop, he said, "Hey, do you mind if I come over to your house for a little while? Both my parents are out."

"Sure," I said, slightly dreading the thought of having to spend the afternoon with Jack pretending I wasn't sad.

But confusion replaced my dread as we entered my house to find both of our moms drinking tea in the kitchen.

"Hey, superstars," my mom said as we approached, "how was school?"

"Good," Jack said breezily, like he hadn't just totally lied to me.

"Jack?" I said suspiciously. "I thought you said your parents were out."

"They are. My dad's at work and my mom's . . . here." He raised his eyebrows at his mom, who coyly sipped her tea.

"Did you ask Mrs. Benning?" Jack asked her.

"I did."

"So I can tell Lou?"

"Go ahead," she replied, winking at my mom.

I looked from Mom to Mrs. Goodrich to Jack—all three of them now grinning at me like idiots.

"Tell me *what*?" I demanded, my heart beating fast.

Jack kept grinning as he spoke.

"So . . . remember that text message I got on the bus?"

"About getting a ticket to *Let's Make a Toast!*?"

"Well, that was only *half*-true. My mom actually got *two* tickets." I felt a lump rise in my throat as I realized what he was saying.

"Do you mean . . . ?" I asked, trying not to get weepy.

Jack beamed at me, proud of his trick.

"Yeah—the other ticket is yours. Wanna come to New York with us?"

"Hey, Earth to Lou."

Jack's hand waved in front of my face, snapping me back to reality—if you could call *this* reality. A heavily tattooed man carrying a wavy auburn wig on a Styrofoam head whisked by as I turned to Jack.

"Sorry, what did you say?"

Jack laughed.

"I said, 'Is this what you pictured a Broadway backstage would look like?'"

"Oh," I said, looking around in wonder for the eight millionth time. "Sort of? I mean, not really, but maybe? I don't know," I stammered, nervously gripping my winter coat, "but it's amazing."

"The St. James Theatre actually has a larger backstage than most," Jack explained to my astonishment. *There were places that were even smaller than this?*

I watched in fascination as the actors nimbly maneuvered past us through the narrow corridor, loosening neckties and pulling bobby pins from their wigs. Only minutes ago these same people had been *onstage*, singing and dancing in front of an ecstatic crowd. The show had been better than I'd hoped, with songs that would be stuck in my head for months. Jack and I had screamed ourselves hoarse during the curtain call. Now all of the people that we'd been cheering for from afar were checking their cell phones and debating which subway lines would get them home fastest. I was feeling awestruck by every single one of them when a newly familiar voice rang out:

"All right, who let these *kids* in here?"

I turned to see Madeleine Zimmer, the star of the show, her eyes twinkling mischievously under her false eyelashes and her Crest-commercial-white teeth lined up in a perfect smile. She wore a long pink-and-red silk kimono, and when Jack jumped into her arms, he disappeared behind its floor-length sleeves.

"Maddie!" His exclamation was muffled by the fabric. "You were *incredible!*"

"Well, once I knew that *Jack Goodrich* was going to be in the audience, I upped my game," she said, releasing him. "Oh my goodness, let me look at you. You got so big!"

Jack looked down at his feet like he'd failed to notice his recent growth spurt.

"Yeah, I guess so," he said with a chuckle.

"And who's this great beauty?" Madeleine asked, gesturing toward me.

Great beauty? She's got to be kidding, I thought. *This woman looks like a supermodel, and I look like . . . well, like a starstruck twelve-year-old theater nerd with hat hair holding a huge parka.*

"This is my best friend from Ohio—Louisa Benning," answered Jack. Normally I would have offered up my nickname; here I was too shy. Jack, however, was not: "But everyone calls her Lou."

"Then Lou is what I will call you, too!" declared Madeleine, and the next thing I knew I was enveloped by those silk kimono sleeves. I almost fainted.

"Come on, I'll show you my dressing room," said Madeleine, and as she turned to lead us up a flight of stairs I started to feel like Alice in Wonderland. Except unlike Alice I felt big and small *at the same time*: big because the stairs kept getting narrower and narrower as we went up, and small because I was still just some nobody kid from Shaker Heights, Ohio. But I wasn't just some nobody, was I?

I was Jack Goodrich's best friend. He had just said it out loud to a real Broadway star, and that alone made me feel one step closer to belonging to this magical world. I felt light-headed. As we reached the top of the stairs, I grabbed the hem of Jack's coat and whispered in his ear, "I know this kind of thing is normal for you, but I am sort of freaking out right now."

"Are you okay?" he whispered back.

"Oh, yeah, it's a good kind of freak-out," I said, peering into Madeleine's dressing room. It was filled with framed photographs, colorful throw pillows, and little potted plants. I smiled, imagining what my own Broadway dressing room would look like someday.

"This might be the coolest night of my life."

Andrew Keenan-Bolger is a musical-theater actor originally from Detroit. He has appeared on Broadway in *Newsies*, *Mary Poppins*, *Seussical*, and *Beauty and the Beast*. Andrew and Kate Wetherhead created the popular web series *Submissions Only*, which was hailed as one of *Entertainment Weekly*'s "Top 10 Things We Love."

Kate Wetherhead originated the role of Chutney in *Legally Blonde: The Musical*. She has performed extensively Off-Broadway and regionally, and was in the Broadway production of *The 25th Annual Putnam County Spelling Bee*.